Rat Wives

AND OTHER PLAYS

by Don Nigro

A SAMUEL FRENCH ACTING EDITION

SAMUEL FRENCH

FOUNDED 1830

NEW YORK HOLLYWOOD LONDON TORONTO

SAMUELFRENCH.COM

ISBN 978-0-573-69636-7   Printed in U.S.A.   #29040

IMPORTANT BILLING AND CREDIT REQUIREMENTS

All producers of *RAT WIVES AND OTHER PLAYS* *must* give credit to the Author of the Play in all programs distributed in connection with performances of the Play, and in all instances in which the title of the Play appears for the purposes of advertising, publicizing or otherwise exploiting the Play and/or a production. The name of the Author *must* appear on a separate line on which no other name appears, immediately following the title and *must* appear in size of type not less than fifty percent of the size of the title type.

CONTENTS

RAT WIVES

CHARACTERS

JANET ACHURCH
MRS PATRICK CAMPBELL
FLORENCE FARR
ELIZABETH ROBINS

SETTING

Backstage at the Avenue Theatre in London on a blustery autumn night in the year 1896. A sofa, some overstuffed chairs, a liquor cabinet, some makeup tables facing downstage, the mirrors invisible, a stray prop or two here and there, some trunks. Comfortable old furniture, just a bit ratty.

RAT WIVES was first produced October 4-8, 2005 at the Perko Playpen Theatre at York University in York, Pennsylvania with the following cast:

JANET ACHURCH. . . . . Sarah Houghton

MRS PATRICK CAMPBELL . . . . Angela Fasanella

FLORENCE FARR . . . . Shannon Fitzgerald

ELIZABETH ROBINS . . . . Jen Miller

Directed by Blake McCullar. Stage Manager, Mark Sixt.

(In the darkness we can hear **JANET**'s *vocal warmups as lights come up on four actresses backstage at the Avenue Theatre in London, late on a blustery night in the autumn of 1896, just before a performance of Ibsen's* Little Eyolf: **JANET ACHURCH**, *tall, blond, and voluptuous;* **ELIZABETH ROBINS**, *a thin, lovely but somewhat prim American;* **MRS PATRICK CAMPBELL**, *a magnificent and formidable theatrical goddess with a charming but sardonic and slightly dangerous manner; and* **FLORENCE FARR**, *delicate and amiable, with a kind of fey, ethereal beauty which is somewhat misleading. The first three are in costume,* **JANET** *to play Rita, the heroine,* **ELIZABETH** *to play Asta, her sister-in-law, and* **MRS PAT** *is touching up her makeup as the Rat Wife, a grotesque character much older than she is.* **FLORENCE** *is their understudy and is in street clothes. She and* **ELIZABETH** *sit one on each end of the sofa.)*

JANET. Well, here's one more billygoat ready to stuff in the barn, as my old whiskery Gramps used to say when commencing to huff and puff his way through another Lear.

MRS PAT. You come from a long line of theatrical people, do you, Janet?

JANET. No, I come from a short line, of which I am most likely the termination point. I did admire old Gramps, though. What a trouper. I asked him once, when he was nearly eighty, backstage taking off his trousers, just how long he was going to keep on doing this, and he said, "Until I get it right, my dear. Until I get it right." A better player than I, alas.

MRS PAT. I thought you were very good last night.

JANET. Did you really think so? I can never tell. You, on the other hand, are always good, and you always know it. I think it was wonderfully unselfish of you to agree to play the Rat Wife. It's not all that common for a celebrated and glamorous West End star like Mrs Patrick Campbell to take on a character role like the Rat Wife simply for art's sake.

MRS PAT. But I adore playing the Rat Wife. There's something about her which I find oddly familiar.

FLORENCE. Perhaps you were a rat wife in a previous life.

ELIZABETH. All wives are rat wives, because all husbands are rats.

FLORENCE. Oh, not all husbands, surely. I think Janet's husband, for example, is quite charming.

JANET. Yes, that's the problem. Every woman in London thinks my husband is charming. Of course, they haven't experienced the exquisite misfortune of being married to him, and neither have you. At least, not to my knowledge, although with Charlie, anything is possible.

(**JANET** *goes to the cabinet, takes out a bottle and glass, and pours herself a drink. The other three exchange brief looks.*)

MRS PAT. Are you drinking, Janet?

JANET. It certainly appears that I am. Do you want some?

MRS PAT. No, thank you. It's just that we thought, I mean, right before the show, after all, and it was our understanding that you'd agreed to –

JANET. I can handle one piddling little drink, for Christ's sake, before the bloody show. You're not my mother, you know, even if you are playing somebody old enough to be.

MRS PAT. I beg your pardon?

JANET. Oh, God, tell me I didn't just say that.

MRS PAT. I'm a year younger than you. And I look it.

JANET. I'm so sorry. I didn't mean to snap at you. Honestly, I didn't. It's just that I'm a bit touchy about the drinking issue at the moment, and when I'm feeling patronized I just blurt out the rudest things before I can stop myself, and doing Ibsen always leaves me in a state of absolute wreckage anyway, and here you've just been complimenting me on my acting, and I've turned on you like a wolverine. Poor stupid Janet.

Always such a struggle to try and impersonate a civil human being. And we four should be more than civil to one another. I mean, we're all women here. We must all stick together, mustn't we?

FLORENCE. Of course we must.

ELIZABETH. Absolutely.

MRS PAT. I am celebrated for my beauty. Do you know how long it takes me to make myself look old and ugly?

JANET. *(taking both* **MRS PAT** *'s hands in hers)* Oh, Stella, please let's be friends. I am desperate, absolutely desperate to be friends, and I respect you so much. Won't you please forgive me?

MRS PAT. Of course, dear. We're all under a great deal of pressure here, doing this uplifting but rather morbid Ibsen play for next to nothing, with the dead child and the crutch floating and such a big, difficult part for you, carrying so much of the load. No wonder you're tense. We're all tense. And yet it's been going rather well, I think.

ELIZABETH. Remarkably well.

FLORENCE. Against all reasonable expectation.

JANET. I'm such an idiot. And you're so understanding. Give me a hug.

MRS PAT. *(backing away just a bit)* Well, you know, hugging is not really my specialty, and I'm just putting on my false nose, and –

JANET. *(Hugging her with great enthusiasm.* **MRS PAT** *looks over Janet's shoulder at the others rather unhappily.)*
Oh, good. Let's all be friends. I mean, really good friends. Let's be sisters.

MRS PAT. Janet, I can't breathe.

JANET. *(letting her go)* Oh, I'm sorry. I hope I didn't crack any ribs. Charles says I'm stronger than a longshore-man. It runs in the family. Mother could crack walnuts between her knees. I'm so glad we're all such good friends. Who says women can't get along in the theatre? A bunch of damned stupid men, that's who.

(She sits on the sofa with one arm around **FLORENCE** *and the other, still holding her drink, around* **ELIZA-BETH**. **FLORENCE** *doesn't really mind, but* **ELIZABETH** *does.* **MRS PAT** *is still recovering from the hug.)*

We can tell each other secrets. We can share intimate backstage gossip with one another. We haven't done that nearly often enough.

ELIZABETH. I never gossip. Gossip is vulgar.

JANET. Of course it's vulgar. That's why it's so much fun. Here's something I've been dying to know. Who among us has actually had sexual intercourse with George Bernard Shaw?

ELIZABETH. Janet, really.

JANET. Oh, come on. Sisters must share useful information. A show of hands, please, for the sake of cast bonding. Who's done the dark deed with GBS?

*(***FLORENCE** *raises her hand.)*

Oh, very good, Florence. Always inspiring to see a woman make a serious contribution to literature.

ELIZABETH. You slept with Shaw?

FLORENCE. I'm afraid so.

ELIZABETH. George Bernard Shaw?

FLORENCE. Guilty.

ELIZABETH. Oh, that's appalling.

FLORENCE. No, it wasn't so bad, actually. Except for a really horrendous case of beard burn on my face. Among other places.

ELIZABETH. Good God.

FLORENCE. Well, it was the only way I could think of to get him to shut up. It didn't work, though. He talked the whole time. He's the only man I've ever known who can do two things at once with his tongue. I don't know how he does it.

ELIZABETH. I can't imagine it. I refuse to think about it.

JANET. That's one of the national characteristics I find most appealing about you Americans. You refuse on principle to think very much about anything.

ELIZABETH. That's not true.

MRS PAT. Yes it is.

FLORENCE. It really is.

JANET. You see? Isn't this fun? We're bonding already.

MRS PAT. Actually, Janet, it's getting on towards curtain time, and –

JANET. Oh, rubbish. We won't go up on time tonight. It's pouring down rain outside. Nobody puts on their rubbers to go see Ibsen. They'd rather stay home and finger the maid. Now, who's had sexual intercourse with Yeats?

(**FLORENCE** *raises her hand.*)

ELIZABETH. Yeats too?

FLORENCE. He's really very sweet, in a clumsy, Irish sort of way.

ELIZABETH. You've slept with George Bernard Shaw and William Butler Yeats?

MRS PAT. My goodness, Florence. I certainly do believe in supporting the arts, but we don't want to overdo it, do we?

FLORENCE. I found them both quite entertaining.

MRS PAT. I find my cocker spaniel entertaining, but I don't want to have intercourse with him.

ELIZABETH. I'm greatly relieved to hear it.

FLORENCE. I wonder why Billy isn't giving us times till curtain? Isn't that his job?

MRS PAT. Billy's probably dead. He's a hundred and four years old if he's a day.

FLORENCE. He's not that old.

MRS PAT. He told me himself he once held Shakespeare's horse.

JANET. All right, then. Who's had intercourse with my husband?

(They all look at **FLORENCE**, *who starts to raise her hand and then abruptly pulls it down.)*

FLORENCE. What are you all looking at? I never slept with Janet's husband.

JANET. You started to raise your hand. I saw it.

FLORENCE. That was merely a reflex action.

JANET. Yes, I imagine a girl who's slept with that many men must have exceptionally well developed reflexes.

FLORENCE. It's not that many. It's only two out of three.

JANET. Two out of the first three names I happened to mention, and you had to think a moment before giving a tentative no on the third one. I'm no mathematical wizard, Florence, but at that rate, it's not only a wonder you find time to pursue your theatrical career, it's a miracle if you can still ride sidesaddle.

ELIZABETH. Janet, please, must you be so very coarse?

JANET. Yes, Elizabeth, I believe I must. I have a profound need to be coarse. You should try it some time. It might do you a world of good. Oh, I suppose it doesn't matter if Florence has slept with my husband. What difference does it make, one more betrayal in the great scheme of things? No man is, after all, that much better or worse than any other.

ELIZABETH. All men are rapists at heart.

MRS PAT. Well, that's not exactly fair. George Bernard Shaw, for one, is no rapist, and he has no heart, to speak of. Shaw is much more like a clever but rather annoying fox terrier. A fox terrier is capable of a number of sins, I have no doubt, but a person is very unlikely to be ravished by one.

JANET. It's interesting that I'm being criticized for coarseness when Stella has just managed to work intercourse with dogs into the conversation twice.

MRS PAT. It's not so much what you say that makes you coarse, but how you say it.

JANET. Oh, ballocks. Who has slept with a fox terrier?

Florence?

FLORENCE. As a child I slept with a sheep dog. But I assure you it was for the most part an entirely Platonic relationship, except for one or two lamentable occasions when the poor creature was in heat.

JANET. My husband is always in heat. I've often thought it would be doing him a great kindness to have him castrated. I know it would take a great load off my mind.

MRS PAT. I must confess, I can't help being a bit curious what it was like, sleeping with Yeats. Was it a mystical experience, allowing him to penetrate your secret rose, as it were?

FLORENCE. Well, I don't know that I'd call it mystical, at least not for me, but he was almost absurdly grateful. I like that in a man.

JANET. I get the impression Florence's rose is not all that much of a secret.

MRS PAT. Shaw, you know, sees the woman as the huntress and the man as the rabbit. Which is actually quite appropriate, at least in his case, as Shaw looks rather like a rabbit – a lewd, carniverous rabbit – although he is a vegetarian, isn't he?

ELIZABETH. I think an arrow through the head would do Shaw a world of good.

JANET. If one makes stew from a vegetarian, is it vegetarian stew?

FLORENCE. Have you really never slept with Shaw, Janet? I know he's immensely fond of you.

JANET. George Bernard Shaw and I have had only spiritual intercourse.

MRS PAT. What the hell does that mean?

JANET. I haven't the faintest idea, but that's what he told me it was.

FLORENCE. He told me he was renouncing spiritual intercourse.

JANET. Well, he must have taken it up again when he heard you were sleeping with Yeats.

ELIZABETH. This man Shaw should really be killed. I'm quite serious. We must take up a collection to hire a reputable assassin. Or, perhaps I'll just cut out the middle man and do it myself. I think I'd rather enjoy it.

MRS PAT. No, dear, we can't have you being strung up for murder. We need you for the play.

ELIZABETH. Then Janet can do it.

JANET. What do you mean, Janet can do it? We don't need me for the play? I've got a bigger part than you do.

FLORENCE. You've got a bigger everything than she does.

MRS PAT. There are no small parts. Although there are some rather small penises.

ELIZABETH. Well, if we can't kill Shaw, can we at least get somebody to make a small incision in his vocal chords?

FLORENCE. Elizabeth, I don't understand why you have such disturbingly violent thoughts about Shaw. He seems harmless enough to me.

ELIZABETH. He's a thoroughly ridiculous and appalling human being.

FLORENCE. Ridiculous, I'll grant you, but not entirely appalling. He has his good points.

ELIZABETH. Name one. I challenge you to say one good thing about Shaw that's not a lie.

FLORENCE. Well, let me think. He plays the piano beautifully.

ELIZABETH. He would like you to believe so, but in point of fact, since he finds himself chronically unable to stop talking, even while he's playing the piano, it's impossible to tell if he's playing well or not. He simply tells you he's playing beautifully and expects you to take his word for it. And he has written me the most inappropriate letters imaginable. He keeps up this absurd pretense that I am in love with him, when in fact I would rather have intimate relations with a dead camel. On one memorable occasion he came pounding on my door in the middle of the night, and invited me to join him in a brisk regimen of naked calisthenics. Luckily, I keep a loaded revolver in the bread box.

FLORENCE. You don't suppose it could be that you're just afraid of men?

ELIZABETH. I'm not at all afraid of men. I simply find them contemptible and more or less idiotic.

JANET. If you think they're idiotic during courtship rituals, wait until you've married one.

ELIZABETH. I did marry one.

MRS PAT. You married a man? How extraordinary. Did you kill him?

ELIZABETH. As it turned out, that wasn't necessary. He killed himself.

JANET. What a surprise.

MRS PAT. Janet.

JANET. Sorry.

ELIZABETH. You needn't be. I wasn't. Well, perhaps I was a little. I was troubled, anyway. I found marriage to be an altogether bizarre experience. But then, of course, he was an actor.

(a loud chorus of groans from the other three)

MRS PAT. Oh, dear.

FLORENCE. Oh, no.

JANET. That was your first mistake.

ELIZABETH. Oh, I know, I know, but in defense of my sanity, he had seemed to be a reasonably happy and fairly well adjusted person, as actors go.

MRS PAT. Well, of course he did.

FLORENCE. They always do.

JANET. They're acting.

ELIZABETH. And then one night, apropos of absolutely nothing, he put on a heavy suit of stage armor, took a walk into the deepest part of the Charles river and drowned himself. I can only conclude that all men are insane.

JANET. What did you do to him?

ELIZABETH. I didn't do anything to him.

FLORENCE. Well, there's your answer.

ELIZABETH. What does that mean?

FLORENCE. How often did you have intercourse?

ELIZABETH. I was suffering from migrane headaches.

FLORENCE. I don't wonder, if you weren't having intercourse.

JANET. Now, why doesn't my husband have the courtesy to go and drown himself? I'd gladly supply the suit of armor.

ELIZABETH. Maybe we could present one to Shaw for Christmas, point him towards the water, and give him a little push.

MRS PAT. I believe Bernard is convinced he can walk on the water.

FLORENCE. If you want Shaw to leave you alone, you're going about it all wrong. The way to get rid of Shaw is to pursue him. Do so and I guarantee you he'll run away shrieking like the Sabine women.

JANET. She's right, you know. Play your cards properly and in no time you can have him galloping into the Thames dressed like the Ghost of Hamlet's Father.

FLORENCE. The real problem with Shaw is that he lives entirely within the confines of his own head.

ELIZABETH. Then how could you do it with him? For that matter, how could you do it with any of them? I mean, do you really like it?

FLORENCE. Well, it's true they do seem to enjoy it quite a bit more than I do, but all in all, I don't mind. I mean, it's good exercise, isn't it? That's what I keep telling myself, anyway. Although I must confess that, on the whole, I would often just as soon be in the Reading Room at the British Museum, studying Babylonian alchemy.

JANET. I've done it at the British Museum. With a Frenchman, behind the Assyrian megaliths. It was quite nice. He was a linguist.

ELIZABETH. But, Florence, don't you ever worry about, you know, consequences?

FLORENCE. I'm an actress. I only believe in consequences on the stage.

ELIZABETH. Yes, but, even so, I mean, with so many lovers –

FLORENCE. It's not so many. Only fifteen.

ELIZABETH. Fifteen? Fifteen?

FLORENCE. I think it's fifteen.

(*She counts on her fingers.*)

Sixteen, if you count Swinburne.

MRS PAT. Swinburne?

FLORENCE. I think sixteen is quite a modest figure, at least when compared to the number of men in London.

MRS PAT. But Swinburne?

JANET. (*getting up to pour herself another drink*) What's wrong with Swinburne?

MRS PAT. Swinburne is like an alcoholic, sadomasochistic garden gnome.

JANET. I like little fellows, myself. They've so much to make up for, they try harder.

MRS PAT. Oh, God, now I'm picturing it. I need a drink.

JANET. (*handing* **MRS PAT** *the drink she's just poured*) Here you go.

MRS PAT. Thank you.

(*She belts it down like she knows what she's doing.*)

Ahh. Just like Mother used to make. I really think that cross-eyed old Billy person should be calling out the time to places. Perhaps he really is dead. Has anybody seen him tonight?

FLORENCE. The last I saw of old Billy, he was in the prop room, nestled between a statue of Venus and a stuffed bear.

MRS PAT. Did he seem to be feeling all right?

FLORENCE. Well, he certainly wasn't feeling any pain. He was snoring like a sailor.

ELIZABETH. Billy drinks more than Janet.

JANET. *(pouring herself another drink)* I think Billy is sweet. Did you know he keeps ferrets? At night when we go home he lets them run about the theatre.

MRS PAT. Those aren't ferrets, dear, those are rats. And he doesn't keep them. He's trying to kill them. Why do you think he keeps that rat poison in the cupboard?

JANET. I thought that was for the playwrights.

ELIZABETH. What I meant about consequences, Florence, was don't you worry about children? The possibility of them, arising as an unexpected consequence of your amorous activities.

FLORENCE. I can't have children.

ELIZABETH. Oh.

(pause)

I'm sorry.

FLORENCE. Yes. Me too.

(pause)

I was married once. Also to an actor. But one day he simply vanished.

MRS PAT. Yes, they will do that, won't they, if you don't nail them to the floor.

JANET. Sometimes you can watch them vanishing right before your eyes.

FLORENCE. I liked him because he was so clean. I think he must have reminded me of my father, who was a great crusader for sanitary water closets.

MRS PAT. How romantic.

FLORENCE. It was, rather. I was studying Shakespeare and tap dancing, and he would pick me nuts in the park. I suppose I should have suspected something was wrong. He did spend rather a lot of time in bed by himself, blowing on his mouth organ and holding long philosophical conversations with the cat. And then one day I looked up and he was gone. I do wish men wouldn't keep falling in love with me. I don't know which is more annoying: when they mean it or when they don't. Not that Shaw wasn't a very amusing talker and Yeats a wonderfully attentive listener, but on the whole, I think I'd just as soon have a parrot.

JANET. Why do we need Elizabeth but not me?

MRS PAT. Pardon?

FLORENCE. Of course, parrots do have a tendency to relieve themselves all over the place, but then, so did Swinburne.

JANET. Why did you say we need Elizabeth for the play, but not me?

MRS PAT. I didn't say that. Elizabeth said that.

ELIZABETH. That's not what I said. And I was joking.

JANET. Elizabeth, you never joke. You have no sense of humor. You're an American.

ELIZABETH. *(gravely)* Americans are a very funny people.

MRS PAT. *(patting* **ELIZABETH** *on the head)* Of course they are, dear.

JANET. Do you consider me expendable?

MRS PAT. Oh, no. We didn't mean that at all. I promise you, we didn't.

(a moment in which nobody will look at **JANET***)*

JANET. What's everybody looking so guilty about? Why will nobody meet my eyes? Come on. Something's up. What's wrong?

MRS PAT. This is probably not the best time to –

JANET. This is the bloody time. Now what the hell is it?

MRS PAT. We've got to go onstage and do this extremely difficult play in a few minutes, and –

JANET. I'm not going anywhere until somebody tells me why nobody will look me in the eye.

(pause)

MRS PAT. If you insist. There was something we needed to speak with you about.

FLORENCE. *(standing up abruptly)* Well, I've got to go. It's time for my yoga.

MRS PAT. Sit down, Florence.

*(**FLORENCE** sits.)*

I suppose the only decent thing is to just tell you straight out, before you hear it from somebody else. The truth is, Janet, that I've been asked to take over your role.

JANET. My role? You've been asked to take over my role?

FLORENCE. *(Standing up again.)* I've just remembered I'm supposed to meet Yeats at a seance, and I've forgotten to bring my Ouija board.

MRS PAT. Florence, sit down now.

FLORENCE. *(Sitting down.)* Oh, this is so horrible.

JANET. You're taking over my role?

MRS PAT. They were to inform you officially of it in the morning. I'm very sorry.

JANET. But you can't do that.

MRS PAT. I'm afraid it's quite out of my hands. It's been decided.

JANET. It's been decided? Who has decided?

MRS PAT. Other persons have decided.

JANET. What other persons?

MRS PAT. Men have decided.

JANET. Men? Men have decided? What men?

MRS PAT. Men with money of course. It's been decided by men with money that we are moving this production to a more lucrative venue, on the condition that I, as a proven West End star, take over your role. It's no reflection on you, dear. You mustn't take it personally. It's purely a business decision.

JANET. But if you take my part, then who's going to be the Rat Wife? Surely they don't expect me to play the Rat Wife.

MRS PAT. Florence is to play the Rat Wife.

JANET. Florence? Florence is the Rat Wife? Florence, is this true?

FLORENCE. Who's had intercourse with Disraeli?

(**MRS PAT** *raises her hand without thinking, then lowers it quickly.*)

JANET. You knew about this, and you said nothing to me?

MRS PAT. I've just told you.

ELIZABETH. Disraeli?

FLORENCE. I need some of that liquor.

(**FLORENCE** *goes over to pour herself a drink.*)

ELIZABETH. Florence, you don't drink.

FLORENCE. Well, I'm starting.

JANET. Elizabeth, did you know about this?

ELIZABETH. I had no idea she'd slept with Disraeli.

JANET. Did you know I was being dropped from the cast?

MRS PAT. Elizabeth is American. She doesn't know anything.

JANET. How could you do this?

ELIZABETH. I don't know. How could she sleep with Disraeli?

JANET. How could you three conspire behind my back –

MRS PAT. Men conspired behind your back. I didn't.

JANET. Oh, ballocks.

MRS PAT. I don't see why we need to keep bringing ballocks into this.

FLORENCE. *(drinking her drink)* Yes. Ballocks has nothing to do with it.

JANET. Ballocks has everything to do with it.

ELIZABETH. Will you people please stop saying ballocks?

JANET. You don't give a fart in a flea circus what men do and you never have. You took the part from me because you wanted it. You always wanted it. That's probably why you agreed to play the damned wretched Rat Wife in the first place, so you could talk them into getting rid of me and steal my part. And Florence can no more play the Rat Wife than she can speak Italian out her buttocks.

MRS PAT. Why can't she?

FLORENCE. I can speak Italian.

JANET. Florence is too damned ethereal to play some dirty, smelly old Rat Wife.

ELIZABETH. Ethereal? She's slept with sixteen men. You call that ethereal?

FLORENCE. Seventeen, if you count Oscar Wilde.

ELIZABETH. Oscar Wilde?

MRS PAT. You're saying I'm not ethereal?

JANET. You're about as ethereal as a horse.

MRS PAT. Well, that wasn't a very nice thing to say.

FLORENCE. It's true, though.

MRS PAT. *(It's finally registering.)* Oscar Wilde?

FLORENCE. Well, it was an experiment. Better him than Disraeli.

MRS PAT. Disraeli was a very sweet man, and much better in bed than Gladstone.

ELIZABETH. I think I'm going to be sick.

MRS PAT. *(handing* **ELIZABETH** *her drink)* Here, have a drink. Maybe it'll loosen you up a little.

*(***MRS PAT** *gets another drink for herself.)*

JANET. You couldn't loosen her up with a grease gun and a socket set. And I don't believe that story about the suit of armor, either. Her husband probably died of exhaustion from trying to pry her legs apart, a problem which three quarters of literary London doesn't seem to have had with Florence.

FLORENCE. A minute ago I was too ethereal.

JANET. A minute ago I had the lead in this play.

MRS PAT. Janet, stop picking on your fellow actors. Florence can't help being a slut any more than Elizabeth can help being American.

ELIZABETH. Will you stop saying that as if it were some sort of unspeakable social disease? Elizabeth can't help having bubonic plague. Elizabeth can't help being the village idiot. Do you have the slightest comprehension of how incredibly, insufferably patronizing you British can be?

MRS PAT. We're not patronizing. We're just culturally superior in virtually every way imaginable. Anyway, I'm half Italian, and thus very much above that sort of thing. Janet, I assure you, I feel just terrible about all this. I really did not intend for this to happen.

JANET. Then why am I being sacked?

MRS PAT. You really don't want to get into this just before a performance. And speaking of that, where the hell is that stupid little son of a bitch Billy, anyway? Is there nobody else in this theatre?

JANET. Screw the performance. And screw Billy. And don't try and tell me what I want, you glorified store manikin. Why was I sacked, if not to gratify your cretinous ambition and bottomless malice?

MRS PAT. My malice is not bottomless. It definitely has a bottom. And I've just told you, if you will take the trouble to give off shrieking and listen for a moment, that some major commercial investors have come forward, and their feeling, as I understand it, is that our production will be a greater success in a commercial venue if a more celebrated performer like myself is playing the lead. I can't help it if I'm celebrated, can I?

JANET. But why just me? Why don't they sack Elizabeth? She's not celebrated. She's an American.

MRS PAT. They can't sack Elizabeth because Elizabeth owns the English rights to the play.

ELIZABETH. I trust that's not the only reason.

MRS PAT. Trust is a wonderful thing.

JANET. Well, Elizabeth, since you own the rights, then you can stop this, can't you? Elizabeth? Can't you stop this?

ELIZABETH. I don't think it's my place to.

JANET. Your place? Why isn't it your place? You own the goddamned rights to the play. Don't you think I'm good enough to perform with you people? Didn't you read my review?

ELIZABETH. Your review was written by George Bernard Shaw, who wants to sleep with you.

JANET. I don't see what difference that makes. Shaw wants to sleep with everybody, except possibly Florence, who's already had that dubious distinction.

FLORENCE. Oh, he still wants to sleep with me, I just won't let him any more. I much prefer Yeats.

MRS PAT. Is Yeats a better lover?

FLORENCE. He's a better writer. If you want a good lover, don't go to the Irish, get an Italian. But then, you know that. You probably slept with Garibaldi.

JANET. Is that really it? You don't think I'm good enough?

ELIZABETH. I think you're a very interesting and passionate actress, with moments of genuine inspiration and occasional brilliance, but your performances, although often exciting, tend to be rather uneven, more or less out of control, and distressingly unreliable.

JANET. Unreliable?

ELIZABETH. Erratic. Interesting but unpredictable.

JANET. At least I don't act with a pole up my ass like you. You're about as animated as a butter churn, and with less sex appeal.

ELIZABETH. Thank you for illustrating my point.

JANET. What point? You don't have a point. You've barely got an ass. You look like a fence post with teeth.

ELIZABETH. Janet, I'm going to stick fast to the high road here and choose not to take umbrage, because I can see that you're becoming inebriated.

JANET. I'm not inebriated. I'm furious but I'm not inebriated. And what difference would it make if I was? Half the actors in England are drunks. Even the great Henry Irving played Richard the Third drunk one night and began issuing audible stage directions to the other actors in blank verse. If we didn't drink, how could we possibly stand being actors? We'd all have hung ourselves a long time ago. This is not about me being inebriated. This is about blind, vicious, stupid jealousy and envy and treachery, abject treachery and betrayal. And you all knew. All three of you knew, and you said nothing to me. You've all been conspiring behind my back. Even you, Florence.

FLORENCE. I haven't conspired behind anything. I've never conspired in my life. And I'm not at all ambitious. Really I'm not. I'm quite happy to be a merely useful actress, as long as I can keep up with my yoga lessons and make it to the occasional seance, even though I generally get the giggles when I make the mistake of glancing over at Yeats. And it is great fun grabbing Willy under the table. I believe in fact that's the chief reason he brings me. What? Have I got off the track? What was I saying?

MRS PAT. Florence, we don't care.

ELIZABETH. What's wrong with my ass? I've got a perfectly good ass. I'd rather have my skinny ass than your fat ass any day.

JANET. I beg your pardon?

FLORENCE. Janet has a beautiful ass. I wish I had her ass.

JANET. You can't have it, but you can kiss it.

MRS PAT. Elizabeth, I believe you've finished your drink. Would you like another?

ELIZABETH. You bet your sweet ass I would.

(**MRS PAT** *pours* **ELIZABETH** *another drink.*)

JANET. I do believe Miss Robins, the great disciple and champion of Ibsen, is getting a bit tipsy.

ELIZABETH. I'm not tipsy. You're the one who's spinning.

JANET. You make such a fuss about your great commitment to art, and all the while you're sneaking about with greasy-fingered West End backers to take this thing I've sweated blood for and turn it into some kind of money making, vapid piece of pig flop. You Americans are all alike.

FLORENCE. No they're not. Some of them have mustaches.

ELIZABETH. All Americans are not alike.

JANET. You are. Your theatre is a whorehouse, and you worship guns and money. Every one of you.

ELIZABETH. I don't worship anything of the sort. And I see this production as a great opportunity to bring Ibsen to the masses.

JANET. Bring Ibsen to my left buttock. You might as well bring chocolates to pigs.

FLORENCE. Who's slept with Ibsen? Stella?

MRS PAT. Oh, shut up, Florence.

FLORENCE. Don't tell me to shut up. I'm the Rat Wife now, and you've apparently slept with all the Prime Ministers back to William Pitt the Elder. You think you're better than us because you're more famous in the West End, but fame is a great load of ballocks and you know it.

ELIZABETH. Why must this conversation always return to ballocks?

MRS PAT. I never said I was better than you or anybody else.

FLORENCE. You married an actor, too. You're just as stupid as the rest of us.

MRS PAT. An actor? What actor? When?

FLORENCE. You're Mrs Patrick Campbell aren't you? Wasn't he an actor?

MRS PAT. Oh, they're all actors. Any man making love is always engaged in some form of puerile stage performance. Professional actors are simply less good at it, so they must go upon the stage in order to find opportunities to make love to pretty women. They are all born lying.

JANET. And you weren't?

MRS PAT. I never lie. I embellish on occasion but I never lie.

JANET. You hypocrite. All three of you are such hypocrites.

How could you do this to me? The treachery. The betrayal.

ELIZABETH. I have not betrayed you. I've never betrayed anyone in my life, and I resent the implication that I would do any such thing.

JANET. Oh, climb down off your damned high horse, Betsy.

ELIZABETH. I don't have a high horse. I once had a rocking horse. Good old Sparky. I miss him. I'd like another drink, please.

MRS PAT. I think you've had enough. You're not used to guzzling hard liquor like Janet is.

JANET. I've had good reason to drink. My whole life has been like this, an apparently endless and certainly pointless series of disasters. I'm like the charge of the bleeding Light Brigade.

MRS PAT. That's what theatre is: one disaster after another, punctuated by the occasional delusion of momentary triumph. Get used to it or get out.

JANET. I can't get out. I've nowhere else to go. This is the only thing I know. Mother died when I was born. Father was an actor, and not a very friendly one. This life is the only thing he left me. My first husband was gone in the blink of an eye. Also an actor. I've always been so hungry for love. I come to the theatre each night looking for it. We all do – that's why we subject ourselves to this unspeakable humiliation night after night. And when a genius like Shaw comes along, compares me favorably to a lighthouse, and tells me I must do Ibsen, I do Ibsen, and look what happens. What a fool I am.

FLORENCE. A lighthouse? What did he mean by that?

JANET. Oh, who knows? He also said he'd like to be strangled in my hair. What the hell did that mean?

ELIZABETH. He told me he wanted me to pet him, buy him candy, and wheel him through Hyde Park in a perambulator. The man's an egomaniacal pervert.

JANET. At least Shaw actually pays attention to a person.

MRS PAT. He doesn't really, you know. He never really leaves his own mind. Even when he's pretending to make love to a woman, it's actually an elaborate form of self-abuse.

JANET. Shaw wouldn't have done to me what you've done. This is it. This is the end for me. My life is over.

MRS PAT. Your life isn't over. Your innocence may be over. Your life continues.

FLORENCE. Janet, I'm very sorry about the role and all, I really am, but, you know, there will be other roles, and you seem to me to have quite a nice life, all in all. I mean, your present husband is really handsome and charming, and he does seem to love you. Some of us would give anything for that.

JANET. Oh, I suppose Charles loves me well enough, but he spends more time with the pawnbroker. There was never a man in the history of the world better at making money vanish. He could have been a great magician. I wish he could make himself disappear. I wish he could make me disappear. I believe I'm going to pass out.

FLORENCE. *(rushing to steady her)* Oh, don't fall over. Nobody here is strong enough to hold you up.

JANET. I nearly died in childbirth, last time, and I've not been well since. The doctors gave me morphia, and it nearly killed me. I wish to God I had some now.

FLORENCE. *(helping* **JANET** *to the sofa)* Come and sit down a moment, Janet, and compose yourself. We really must be be starting the play soon.

JANET. It's theatre that will kill me some day. Charles had the bright idea to take me on a grand theatrical tour of Australia, New Zealand, and Tasmania. All the great Tasmanian theatres. He thought there must be money in it somehow. It turns out they are not particularly big on Shakespeare in Tasmania. I was dreadfully ill, but we had to keep performing to pay our way home. They kept me going with alcohol and morphia until we got back to England, where the doctor informed me that my problem was an addiction to alcohol and morphia. Getting this role was such a great thing for me. And now you've stolen it from me. Stabbed me in the back. Stabbed me in the front. Stabbed me in my big, fat ass.

MRS PAT. It's a shame you've had a difficult time of it, Janet, but none of us has had it all that easy, and the fact remains –

JANET. The fact remains that I am doing the best work of my life here, in this wretched, dismal, wonderful clat-farting play, so of course you all feel compelled to conspire with a bunch of damned men to betray me so you can get rich dragging poor old Ibsen off kicking and screaming to the West End. We're doing a great thing here. We're doing Ibsen, difficult, boring, drab, cranky old Ibsen, and we're doing it as well as anybody has ever done it in the history of the world, and the first chance you three stupid whores get to cut my throat and take my part away and ruin it all, you jump at it, so goddamned anxious to make yourselves slaves once again to those greedy West End bastards with money in their pockets and shit between their ears. Aren't you the least bit ashamed of yourselves?

FLORENCE. I'm ashamed, but not of that. Well, actually, perhaps it is that.

MRS PAT. Janet, we don't wish you any ill whatsoever, we really don't. We're all extremely fond of you. But this is theatre, and we're actors. You know what theatre is like. We can't be expected to behave honorably on every possible occasion. If we do, we'll be devoured. We've simply got to look after ourselves. If we don't, nobody else will. You know you'd do the same thing, if the situation were reversed. In fact, you did, didn't you?

JANET. I would not. I would never do any such thing.

ELIZABETH. Oh, come on, Janet. We know what you did.

JANET. I have no idea what I did. What did I do?

ELIZABETH. You went behind our backs to try and negoti-
ate your own West End contract.

JANET. I might have spoken to some people, yes. I speak
to a lot of people. Why shouldn't I? It's not the same
thing at all. I didn't conspire to take anybody's part
away. I was quite happy to take you all to the West End
with me, even Florence.

FLORENCE. Well, thank you very much.

JANET. *(looking at* **ELIZABETH**, *realizing)* Oh, my God. So they
went to you, as owner of the English rights, and you
sold me out.

ELIZABETH. I merely mentioned to Mrs Campbell that
it had come to my attention you were negotiating
secretly to play this role in the West End.

JANET. And she talked them into giving her my part instead.

ELIZABETH. You started it, Janet.

JANET. I didn't take her part. She took mine. She could
have kept playing the damned Rat Wife until dooms-
day for all I cared. But she wasn't satisfied with that.
She had to take what was mine. To take for herself all
that I had. All that meant anything to me in the world.

MRS PAT. Oh, please, don't lurch into dramatics on us.
You forget we are a somewhat jaded audience here.
We've seen all your tricks and stolen half of them from
one another. What happened was simply that in the
course of my conversations with these people, the subject of me playing Rita came up, I don't recall exactly
how, and they seemed quite excited by this prospect.
I did not encourage them, but they were adamant,
once they'd got the idea into their heads. You know
how men are. One head, one idea. To have a second
idea they'd need a second head. If it isn't sex, food or
murder then it's money. And I was certainly not about
to turn such an opportunity down, especially since we
knew you'd been conspiring behind our backs long
before we conspired behind yours. As you well know,
these opportunities don't come along every day. If you

don't grab them by the ballocks when they appear, you may never get another pair of ballocks to grab, ever again. And, frankly, Janet, the naked truth is, they were already rather disenchanted with you, my dear. They found you a trifle – unstable.

JANET. *(rushing at* **MRS PAT***)* I'll show you unstable, you two-faced, posturing gorgon.

FLORENCE. *(Rushing to get between them.)* Stop it. Janet, calm down.

JANET. She's a monster.

MRS PAT. I am not any sort of monster. Suppose they'd wanted to keep you and replace Elizabeth. Would you have given up your chance and stood up for her?

JANET. That's different.

ELIZABETH. How is it different?

JANET. Well, for one thing, I'm actually good.

ELIZABETH. I'm good. I'm excellent.

JANET. How excellent can a person be with a flag pole up her ass?

ELIZABETH. There is nothing up my ass. Would you like to take a look?

JANET. If you don't believe me, just ask Shaw.

ELIZABETH. I'm happy to say that George Bernard Shaw knows nothing whatsoever about my ass, and never will. He apparently knows something about Florence's ass.

FLORENCE. Oddly enough, although not at all a religious person, Shaw actually prefers the missionary position. In these matters he is for the most part as conventional as his dramatic structure.

ELIZABETH. I could have gone quite happily through life not knowing that. Oh, God, now I'm picturing it again. I need more liquor.

MRS PAT. I really don't think we should be drinking any more.

ELIZABETH. You've been lapping it up like a horse at a water trough.

MRS PAT. I know what I'm doing. You've spent your life with a flag pole up your ass.

FLORENCE. You're right, Janet. You are good. You're very good. You're a bit uneven, but you've got more inside you than any of us, I think.

MRS PAT. Speak for yourself, Florence.

FLORENCE. I always speak for myself. Who else could I speak for? I'd give anything to have Janet's energy and magnetism and power onstage. That's exactly why I know she'll be all right.

JANET. Well, that makes me feel much better. The whore of Babylon thinks I'll be all right. The new Rat Wife praises my animal magnetism as she pulls her rapier out from my backside.

FLORENCE. Janet, how could I pass up a chance at a meaty character role like the Rat Wife? Do you think I enjoy sitting back here all night as a thoroughly useless understudy, knitting a three-armed cardigan, while you three are onstage every night tearing up the scenery with your teeth?

ELIZABETH. I've never torn up anything with my teeth, although once, as a child, I did bite the cat. But she bit me first.

FLORENCE. My life has not signified much up to this point. I've spent the greater part of it in a fruitless search for truth. I've studied Egyptology and alchemy, spiritualism, Babylonian astrology and theosophy. I've played cribbage with Madame Blavatsky and quoits with Aleister Crowley and I am Praemonstratrix in the Order of the Golden Dawn. I am a very serious person. And yet here I am, stuck backstage knitting sweaters for the Elephant Man. I want more out of life.

MRS PAT. *(beginning to feel her liquor)* I understand Aleister Crowley has a remarkably small penis. Is that true?

JANET. Have you found it?

FLORENCE. Aleister Crowley's penis?

JANET. The truth. You've spent your life searching for the truth. Have you found it, or anything like it?

FLORENCE. Of course I haven't found it. But I've met a

great many intensely peculiar people along the way. The road to truth is like a freak show carnival. I've never actually seen Aleister Crowley's penis, despite the fact that he's gone pretty far out of his way to show it to me on several occasions, once in the middle of Trafalgar Square.

MRS PAT. Lord Nelson had a rather small penis as well.

ELIZABETH. Did you sleep with Lord Nelson too?

MRS PAT. *(Drinking.)* Don't be ridiculous. I slept with Napoleon. His penis was so miniscule I had to send out a search party. In my experience, the more a man worships violence, the smaller his penis.

ELIZABETH. Can we stop talking about penises? Let's go back to ballocks.

JANET. My life is over.

MRS PAT. Your life is not over. For God's sake, it's only a play.

JANET. My life is not a play.

MRS PAT. I didn't say your life was a play. Although probably your life is a play. You certainly live it like a play, all sound and fury, signifying very little. I mean that theatre is like love. One play ends, another begins.

JANET. So help me, if you start getting philosophical on me I shall break this bottle and cut my throat with it.

MRS PAT. Really, Janet, must you be so theatrical?

JANET. Of course I must. I'm a bloody actress, aren't I?

MRS PAT. Precisely why you shouldn't waste theatrics on real life, which is trivial at best and quite often perfectly unspeakable. Save the good stuff for your work.

JANET. I have no work. You've just stolen my work. This is my work and you've taken it from me.

MRS PAT. It's just one role. Is it really worth all this anguish?

JANET. Which way do you want to have it, Stella? Either art is trivial or life is. You're speaking out of both sides of your mouth.

MRS PAT. Well, of course I am. When life proves unsatisfactory, one retreats into theatre. When theatre betrays one, as it inevitably does, one simply escapes back into

life. This way one always has a place to go. It's like
having a house in the city and one in the country. You
can't allow yourself to become suicidal every time the
plumbing bursts in one of your houses. Just move to
the other one until you can get it fixed.

JANET. What if you only have one house in a rather bad
neighborhood, and the plumber never shows up, and
your husband is in Brighton fornicating with an eigh-
teen year old contortionist?

MRS PAT. Well, that's a very sad case, and an even sadder
metaphor, but nevertheless, my dear, one must never
despair. I forget why.

JANET. It's no use. Nothing is any use. I'd have commit-
ted suicide a long time ago but I haven't been able
to decide on an aesthetically satisfying way of doing
myself in. I hate guns because a gun is such a terrible
prop to have in a play. You show them the gun in the
first act, and in the third act somebody blows their
brains out. How tedious. And I can't stand the sight of
blood, ever since I saw your perfectly dreadful performance in the Scottish play.

MRS PAT. I was a spectacular Lady Mac. I can't help it if
Forbes-Robertson plays everything like a mortician.

JANET. On the whole, I suppose poison would be the least
unsatisfactory method. Do we still have that bottle of
whatever it was old Billy was using on the rats?

MRS PAT. You don't want to take rat poison. Believe me, I
know about these things. I'm the Rat Wife.

JANET. No, you're not the Rat Wife. Florence is the Rat
Wife. You're the great West End star, and I'm the
Shakespeare Queen of Tasmania.

(She rummages around at the bottom of the cupboard.)

I believe it's in here somewhere.

MRS PAT. You don't need any more liquor.

JANET. Not liquor. Rat poison.

FLORENCE. Billy doesn't keep rat poison in the liquor cabinet.

JANET. *(pulling out a blue bottle with xxx on it)* Here it is. Good old Billy. I knew he was good for something. I'll just put some of this in my drink. That should do it nicely.

(JANET pours some of the contents of the blue bottle into her drink.)

FLORENCE. Janet, what are you doing?

JANET. *(stirring the drink with her finger)* Putting rat poison in my drink. Gives it a nice fizz, actually. I feel a bit like Dr Jekyll.

FLORENCE. *(rushing over to take the drink from JANET)* Give me that.

JANET. Hey. Get your own poison, Flossie.

(JANET starts to lick the finger she stirred the drink with.)

ELIZABETH. *(holding Janet's arm away from her face to keep her from licking the finger)* Don't lick your finger.

JANET. Why? Do you want to lick it?

ELIZABETH. No, I don't want to lick your finger.

JANET. George Bernard Shaw wants to lick my finger.

ELIZABETH. George Bernard Shaw wants to lick everybody's anything.

JANET. He wants to paint faces on my toes and give them names and kiss them one by one.

ELIZABETH. Help me, somebody. She's as strong as an ox.

FLORENCE. *(putting down the poisoned drink and rushing over to help)* Janet, stop it. Stella, for God's sake, help us.

MRS PAT. *(drinking)* Oh, please. It's merely histrionics.

JANET. Give me back my finger. I need my finger to punctuate exclamations and plug orifices.

ELIZABETH. *(despite Florence's help, still having a terrible time keeping Janet's finger away from her mouth)* Stop it. Will you stop it?

MRS PAT. Children, children. Try and play nicely.

(Producing a handkerchief, strolling over rather

majestically and wrapping it around Janet's finger, then grasping the finger in her palm and sliding the handkerchief off, thus removing the poison.)

MRS PAT. *(cont.)* And there we have it.

FLORENCE. I can see you've done that before.

MRS PAT. I've done everything at least twice.

JANET. You people are horrible.

ELIZABETH. We've just saved your life.

JANET. You've ruined my life, and now you won't even let me put an end to myself. You want me to suffer as long as possible. Why can't you just let me have my drink?

MRS PAT. You really shouldn't drink, Janet. It's bad for your figure. What's left of it.

*(**MRS PAT** belts down her own drink.)*

JANET. Oh, God, I want to die.

*(**JANET** lunges for the poisoned drink, which **FLORENCE** has put down on the cabinet.)*

FLORENCE. Don't let her have that.

MRS PAT. *(snatching the poisoned drink up before **JANET** can get it)* No. Bad girl. Bad.

JANET. Give me that. Give it to me.

MRS PAT. *(Who now has her own drink in one hand and the poisoned one in the other, holding them both away from **JANET**.)* I'm sorry, Janet. I always do what Florence says. Just like Willy Yeats, Bernard Shaw and half the male population of the Western Hemisphere.

JANET. George Bernard Shaw is a loathesome, mustachioed little piss ant, and so are you.

MRS PAT. *(holding both drinks up above her head)* Here, now. If you're going to become scurrilous I shall be forced to pour your hemlock in the aspidistra.

JANET. Oh, don't waste it. Drink it yourself, why don't you?

ELIZABETH. *(trying to keep **JANET** away from **MRS PAT**)* Give it to Shaw. You'll be the toast of London.

MRS PAT. Actually, that's not a bad idea. We could murder Shaw and blame Janet. The perfect crime.

JANET. I don't want to kill Shaw. He thinks I'm a lighthouse.

MRS PAT. Here's a riddle. How can you tell if George Bernard Shaw is really dead, or just shamming? Answer, if he's not talking, he's dead.

ELIZABETH. *(with* **FLORENCE**, *managing to drag* **JANET**, *one by each arm, over towards the sofa)* Come on, Janet. Let's sit down a moment. You're making me dizzy.

FLORENCE. I think it's a horrible idea, murdering Shaw. I mean, what would we do with the body?

(**ELIZABETH**, **JANET** *and* **FLORENCE** *all collapse at once on the sofa,* **JANET** *in the middle, the other two holding her arms, kerplunk.)*

ELIZABETH. We could throw him in the Thames.

JANET. He'd sink like a rock. There's not an ounce of fat upon his body.

(The other three look at her.)

So I've heard, at any rate.

FLORENCE. I can't have you being so miserable, Janet. It torments me so. You carry a powerful cloud of grief around with you and it infects everybody.

JANET. You should be tormented. You've all betrayed me shamefully.

FLORENCE. I suppose we have, haven't we? I mean, really, there's no getting round it. We really are horrible people. Although, to be fair, we're probably not much more horrible than people in general. The world is made of betrayal. Men betray women, women betray men, and women are always quite ready to betray other women, aren't they? Particularly actresses. We're the worst. We're always betraying somebody. It's the play-acting. We're trained to lie. That's why people don't respect us.

MRS PAT. People respect us. They worship us.

FLORENCE. They may worship us but they don't really respect us. Anyway, nobody worships me, except perhaps for Willy Yeats, and he's prepared to worship any reasonably nice looking woman if she'll allow him. It's not even the copulation that really matters, although he does rather like that, but just being permitted to worship will do. He's quite insane.

JANET. All men are insane.

ELIZABETH. All men should be killed.

MRS PAT. Elizabeth, we are civilized people. We don't kill creatures merely for being stupid and worthless.

JANET. Yes we do.

FLORENCE. It's useless to blame men.

JANET. Sheep, for example.

FLORENCE. Men are not the problem.

JANET. Sheep are stupid, and we kill them.

MRS PAT. But sheep are not worthless. Sheep can be eaten.

ELIZABETH. Of course men are the problem.

JANET. I suppose men could be eaten.

FLORENCE. No. The problem is seldom where it actually shows up. The problem is usually earlier than that, in what leads up to where it shows up, in the set up to the punch line, as it were, the preparation for the climax. This is true of dramaturgy but also of life. Willy Yeats taught me that. He's quite intelligent when he's not in love. But he's always in love.

JANET. I don't want to be worshipped. I should like to be loved. Or at the very least, not betrayed every five minutes. I am the sheep, and you've just cut my throat and hung me on a meat hook.

FLORENCE. We don't betray each other because of men. We betray each other because betrayal lurks at the core of human desire like the rot inside an old potato.

JANET. I am an old potato, and you've made me into soup.

MRS PAT. Oh, come on, Janet. Snap out of it and stop feeling sorry for yourself. Theatre is not for sissies, despite what you may have heard.

FLORENCE. I used to think what we do was a kind of holy thing.

JANET. Cows. We kill cows. I am an old cow.

FLORENCE. And I still believe in my heart that it's a holy thing, in the way that copulation is a holy thing, but I think this is not the holiness which brings one's soul to rest.

JANET. A bullet to the head would do that.

FLORENCE. No, no, it would only bring torment in the after life.

JANET. And that would be different than this how?

FLORENCE. The only real satisfaction comes in renunciation.

JANET. There is no satisfaction. There is only, now and then, the escape into the other, which is love, or, in the absence of that, theatre.

FLORENCE. Life is suffering. Suffering is caused by desire. Eliminate desire and you eliminate suffering.

MRS PAT. How does one eliminate desire?

FLORENCE. Follow the eightfold path.

MRS PAT. And what is that?

FLORENCE. I have no idea. I always get lost on the eightfold path. The eightfold path is a labyrinth, rather like the sephiroth of the cabala.

JANET. Rats. We kill rats. Just like the Rat Wife.

ELIZABETH. Where the hell is Billy? Why hasn't he called us?

JANET. The Rat Wife's real name is Mother Lupus. She turns to a werewolf at night. Go and play in the garden, they told me.

ELIZABETH. Florence, why don't you go and check on Billy, and see what's going on out there?

JANET. Have you any troublesome thing that gnaws inside your house? The Rat Wife will be happy to get rid of it.

FLORENCE. Why me? Why don't you go yourself?

JANET. Sometimes you have no choice. You've got to bury your teeth in the crab apple, no matter how sour and wormy it is.

FLORENCE. What's the matter, Elizabeth? Are you afraid to go outside that door?

JANET. All the hungry little baby rats.

FLORENCE. Are you afraid if you go out there, nobody will be there? No audience, nothing, just an empty theatre in the rain?

JANET. There is something moving in the Rat Wife's bag.

ELIZABETH. I'm not afraid of anything. I just think it's very peculiar that nobody has come to tell us what's going on. It really is rather as if we've been forgotten here.

FLORENCE. At some point, we will be forgotten, of course.

JANET. A crazy old hag, dangling a dog in a sack.

MRS PAT. I will not be forgotten.

JANET. She brings the smell of death into the house.

FLORENCE. But you will be forgotten, Stella. Even you. All of us will.

JANET. We have to because we don't want to, and then we drown.

FLORENCE. At some point in the future, sooner than we like to believe, there will be nobody alive on earth who has the slightest idea who any of us was.

JANET. Every single one.

MRS PAT. That's absurd. Nobody's forgotten Shakespeare.

FLORENCE. Eventually they will.

JANET. The crutch is floating.

MRS PAT. Florence, you are a very morbid person.

JANET. The Rat Wife is God.

MRS PAT. And Janet, by the way, what the devil have you been going on about?

JANET. The Rat Wife is God.

MRS PAT. What the hell does that mean?

ELIZABETH. Billy is out there. I know he's out there. He's lurking in the shadows, waiting for us.

MRS PAT. The Rat Wife isn't God. The Rat Wife is an old

woman who lures rats to their death.

JANET. And children.

MRS PAT. And children.

JANET. And actors.

MRS PAT. That's not in the script.

JANET. I'm pregnant.

MRS PAT. Janet, this is no time to be pregnant.

JANET. Nevertheless.

MRS PAT. Oh, dear.

(pause)

Do you know, I've forgotten which one of these glasses is poison.

JANET. They're both poison. Everything is poison.

MRS PAT. All right. Elizabeth, go out there and see what's happened to Billy.

ELIZABETH. I don't see why it should be my job to –

MRS PAT. *(Lady Mac.)* Just go and do it.

ELIZABETH. All right.

(She starts out, comes back.)

Janet, I'm sorry. I'm happy about the child. I'm sorry about the rest. I am sorry.

*(**ELIZABETH** turns to the door, gathers her courage, and starts out.)*

Oh, Billy? Billy? Are you out there?

*(**ELIZABETH** disappears into the darkness. From off:)*

Are you dead? Is everybody dead? Is anybody out there?

FLORENCE. I do hope Billy isn't waiting on the other side of the door with a carving knife. Perhaps he's gone mad and killed the audience.

JANET. The Rat Wife is God and Billy is Jack the Ripper.

MRS PAT. In point of fact, my husband is not an actor. And that also is just as likely to be a tragedy. And I have children, and that too is just as likely to be a tragedy. Or a comedy. Or some bizarre mixture of both. I cannot always defend the way I behave. I am only trying to be alive before I am dead, be young before I am old, be beautiful before I am ugly. We are all playing desperately at the edge of the darkness. But there is never any good excuse for giving another unnecessary pain. I am very sorry I have caused you any distress. I am genuinely sorry.

(Pause. Then **ELIZABETH** *returns.)*

ELIZABETH. It's places for act one. Billy's been huddled on the other side of the door all this time, terrified to come in. With all the screaming, he thought we were tearing one another to pieces in here. These poor little men. They're so easily frightened. The house came late, because of the rain, but it's nearly full now, and they're just about to mutiny. We've got to go on, and we've got to do it right now.

MRS PAT. Janet, it's time to go on.

JANET. You do it. You're going to take my role anyway. Start tonight. You will take my role and Florence will be the Rat Wife and that will be that.

MRS PAT. Rubbish. It's your role for tonight, at least, and what you are going to do, my dear, is go out there and play your part.

JANET. Oh, God, what does it matter? It's just one more performance.

MRS PAT. Any performance could very well be our last. There is no certainty in this place. No assurance of anything. It can all vanish at any moment. We must play each time as if it were our last. Well, maybe this is your last. If it is, then all the more reason to go out and play the damned thing for all you're worth.

JANET. I can't.

MRS PAT. Of course you can.

JANET. I've been drinking.

MRS PAT. We've all been drinking. The audience has been

drinking. God has been drinking. It doesn't matter.

JANET. It's impossible.

MRS PAT. Of course it's impossible. It's always been impossible. It will always be impossible. Do it anyway. We all insist, don't we? Elizabeth?

ELIZABETH. Yes.

MRS PAT. Florence?

FLORENCE. Absolutely.

(Pause. JANET looks at them.)

JANET. Yes, well, help me up, then. Here's one more billy goat to stuff in the barn.

(FLORENCE and ELIZABETH help her up. She's a little wobbly.)

Time to go out once again into the dark. Billy, you ridiculous little son of a bitch, here I come.

(JANET goes out into the darkness.)

ELIZABETH. Is she going to be all right, do you think?

MRS PAT. Oh, who the hell knows?

(She goes to the two drinks, picks up one.)

FLORENCE. Stella, are you sure that's not the poisoned one?

MRS PAT. I'm never sure, my dear. Now, let's go out there and give these poor stupid bastards what they paid for. The Rat Wife has spoken.

(She drinks the drink down. Blackout.)

RHIANNON

CHARACTERS

MERLIN RHYS

MERLIN RHYS.

Rhiannon was her name
always in my head
one green eye, one brown
and choirs of birds in the orchard
in dappledy gray sky the king of nowhere
May eve it was and although since then
there was frail Proserpina and wicked Magdalena
not to mention that little cross-eyed albino woman
in Nanty Glo which is not however to the point
because Wales it was and me a young fool
apprentice village idiot, Ma said, but
Rhiannon always Rhiannon naked
and covered in blood in my head
and screaming, the great clawed hand
come in the window and no don't think of that
think of no not that either, think of yaks
or the baying of red-eared hounds
because King George DeFlores was a fellow
I saw once before in Wales who was
not in fact how do you say
a proper gypsy person but was
throwed out of the gypsies or never was
a gypsy and anyhow not an individual
very much given to the expression
of much affection ordinarily besides us being

later the proprietors of rival American
travelling carny wagon establishments,
and having as he did that wife, that Belladonna,
what a frightening woman that one was,
scare the balls off a pawn shop,
and her pretty frail thing of a big-eyed sister
that Proserpina whom King George DeFlores
could not of course keep his hairy-knuckled
claws off her pretty dimpled arse
for two minutes and so when Belladonna
found the sister naked and with child
by old King George she wouldn't stop
screeching at him at the top of her lungs
until the poor bastard left the sister
by the side of the road to die,
it all goes back to many years ago
whether you want it to or not
when I was a boy in Glamorgan,
sitting on the hill amongst the ruins
of Pendragon Castle
throwing rotten apples at ravens
where Ma said once we was minstrel-kings
or something big I disremember
and there on her pale horse came riding
through the orchard through the broken trees
and sweet-rot apple piles Rhiannon
shimmering young girl riding
like a goddess through the appled twilight
her hair billowing like sails behind her
and my life never meant anything after
but Rhiannon riding there, and her hair,
but the more you chase her
the further away she gets from you
which is how she was, I said

to the angel who came whispering
in my head that night the thing was born
I said to him, oh, but her breasts,
her breasts, oh God, her breasts
but then the giant clawed hand
come clutching in the window
scaley clawed thing hand of God knows what
and Rhiannon all bloody and naked
but that was before in Wales and
where do you come from, I said,
and where are you going, I said,
and what is that thing you have there
in that bag, he said,
at the crossroads by the windmill,
and I said, it's a badger, I said
that's why it squirms around like that
Rhiannon screaming naked on the bed
a sacrifice the angel said
to the Lord of blood and flesh
for I am the book of moonlight lost
she said, don't think of that,
but it's always a war, for memory
being located in the back of the head
whereas imagination of course lies in the front
and reason in the middle, crushed to death
like a roach between I said to the angel
why am I tormented why is my
face devoured by rats but you sees
the most instructive hallucinations
by the exercise of the faculty
of imaginative dementia,
which busies itself not with fictions
but with subtle realities
and sometimes wart hogs.

You could be just like me, said the angel,
if you listen to the right voices.
But creatures get in the way,
and Rhiannon's breasts in candle light –
no, no, wart hogs, wart hogs –
Bel at the pump organ –
You has the power within you, says the angel,
to see what I do, just lather up your
generative faculty in the corn crib
till you hit a state of weasel frenzy
and in the calm that follows
anything is possible.
Him and God was speaking of this
only the other day, he says. God has
some very stubborn opinions – his tastes
being Pagan, but not sufficiently Gothic.
So I told King George DeFlores who says to me
in Maryland (yow yow yow the bats flap around
my head – get away, pump organ, wart hogs)
if I was to leave this poor weeping slut
Proserpina along the road, abandon her
in a ditch, say, on the side of the road to die
near Mary's Grove, he says,
as my hideous terrifying gorgon wife
Belladonna insists, could you come along
after we cross the horizon, as it were,
in the penumbra of our passing wreckage,
and pick up the waif and care for her
and the bastard thing that's about to crawl
out from between her pretty legs?
And I says what the hell do you think I am?
A question the answer to which I'm not
entirely certain I could formulate
if he was to turn it back on me and,

sucking on his cigar, reply, I don't know,
Merlin, what the hell are you?
And what was that thing in the bag
by the way, at the windmill by the crossroads,
in Glamorgan I saw you carrying that night?
And then Rhiannon in my head, her lips,
kissing her lips, and the thing in the bag,
badger, pale horse, and clop of her hooves,
and around the side of the wagon watching then
I sees a little ghostly girl of a creature,
sucking its fist and staring at me in the dusk
one green eye, one brown,
and I hears myself saying yes, all right, I will,
and King George DeFlores looks at me
with tears in his eyes like a grateful dog
and he gives me his windmill ring,
a mystical object which I'd have bet my dick
they'd have to cut off his hand to get from him,
and which I had for years in my pocket until
it fell out a hole and a chicken must
have swallowed it by the pump organ,
Bel said, but it doesn't signify because
I disbelieve in matter anyways. See Bishop Berkeley
for the working out of the poultry logic of that,
or Billy Blake, who was walking down Cheapside
one Sunday with the missus and of a sudden
takes off his hat and bows low, because
he sees the Apostle Petey, having a
anteprandial circumgyration with
Swedenborg in a parrot suit
on the way to a printing house in hell,
which is where all the big ones is,
to see the method by which knowledge
is transmitted from one generation

of snakes to the next when I
was brutally attacked by a vicious pack
of recondite iconographies.
And so our wagons come around the bend
and there was the creature by the side of the road
her stomach round with child, but fey
and beautiful, and her eyes,
looked through me like the eyes
of a owly marmoset, and I was
doomed, of course, old weakness, lost.
It was like when I was a boy in Wales
and peeing in the woods I saw
a tree full of angels like pelicans flapping
and dripping blood from their wings,
and fool that I was, went home and told
my Pap the tale, and was beat to apple sauce
for lying – my first encounter with advanced
literary criticism and blood in my eyeballs.
So when I saw a family of bare-breasted fairy
sisters washing each other in the marshpond
I kept that one to myself, for when you can see
more than others can, they think you're insane,
or lying, or both, but there's always a mirror on
the obverse, bet on it, Ruddy, I says, that time
the dumbass picked up the skunk.
And so, although I was horrified
by the fragile beauty of the thing in the ditch,
I took her in, and gave her soup and made
her laugh by standing on my head,
she was a simpleton, really, but somewhat
magical, and I had begun much against my will
to start feeling barnacley towards the girl,
when the kid pops out in scarlet wailing childbed
clawing its way to the light, and Proserpina

the fey little mother dead in all the mess,
and here I am left with a bloody, shitty,
shrieking little creature thing, a girl
which I was sorely tempted to take out
and throw in the well, since all living things
is always harmful to visions, but the voice
of Rhiannon in my head is whispering, moaning,
kissing, teasing, begging, ordering, singing,
laughing, confusing my wiser instincts,
one green eye, one brown,
so I let the thing live, trying to ignore
the rat tooth gnawing premonition that
I'd become attached again to this damned monster,
attachment being always fatal to
both parties and often to innocent bystanders
as well. And it was. For the creature, Magdalena,
grew up almost as lovely as her mother,
but less gentle, with a temper,
and a wicked humor in her,
cut your throat with sharp remarks, that one,
tolerable enough as a child on my lap,
but when she matured a thing in my head went off
and I began to think of how to leave her
alongside of the road, but she was stubborn
like her father, when she saw a thing
she wanted, and she wanted me, God knows
why she would, I guess she had nothing else
but freaks and animals, and she wouldn't let
me be until in desperation I
finally give up and did the right thing,
which is always a disaster, that is,
I married her, with a one-eyed preacher and
all the trimmings and gizzards.
But that wouldn't satisfy her.

She wanted copulation as well.
And when I said no she would tease me
while I banged my head on the pump organ,
and at last of course let her have it,
and when she was got with child,
which I warned her I was against,
as I knew it would kill her, too,
like it killed her mother before her,
but Magdalena just threw apples at me,
and the child was born in a crab apple orchard,
a boy, and I waited for her to die, but
she didn't, she laughed at me for the tears
I shed. And so when the next one come,
which was my crazy daughter Bel,
I had been somewhat lulled at last into
a false sense of security, which is
in fact the only kind, and damn if she didn't
up and die then. That was Mag.
Keep me off balance right to the end,
that was her. And there I was
left with a bucket of grief and
her two little monkey children,
Rudd and Bel, the boy dumb as a stump,
the girl as mad as a barrel of rats,
and what the hell I was going to do with them,
damned if I knew, but there you are,
and Rhiannon in my head, and the owls
in the orchard woodyard lost at pumpkin time
and the stars in the dark and the owls
and in my dreams Rhiannon on horseback riding
the nightmare onward into the sea's embrace.
I was warned by the angel of this.
The trouble begins when you put yourself
in the other person's head

which some call love but I call lunacy,
looking at the moon like a fool at the goddess
Rhiannon I was howling when the great
claw hand comes in the window and they says
she killed her baby for she was all naked and bloody
but she says, no, a great claw hand come in
the window all scaley and awful but nobody believed her
but me because I knows there's people on the moon
which the angel whispered in my head while I
was squatting in deadly nightshade in the woods
and once when she was very angry at me
Magdalena burned most of my alchemical treatises
I was writing and thus perished
the book of moonlight and much else
and I should have killed her then
and saved myself the later agony
of watching her die, but the boy
was watching Rudd was watching and she
was already big with the next one and
I remembered her simpleton mother
and Rhiannon naked and the thing in the bag
because there are always them who create
and them who destroy and the battle
between them is always as bitter as hyssop
for all creators like all gods
is always hated especially when
they is worshipped and all of them's
eventually murdered by cannibal pygmies although
it all turns out right in the end as the dead poet says.
So put her out of my head I try to fill up
between my ears with lapidaries and pickle makers,
swaddling clothes and head puddings,
but nothing helps for every breath is treason
because heaven and hell are in a woman

and also several buckets of oysters
for woman like the making of images
is a curse for which I am grateful and damned
from Malkuth to Jehosaphat for what
allows us to guess what is inside the heads
of other people without actually taking a spoon
and scooping out the brain is a curse like art
or death or hemlock soup and then as I
drift off to somewhere else she is there again
Rhiannon tied to a post there naked by
the muddy lane and stoned in our village
them screaming at her, murderess, murderess,
but she said no, it was a big claw hand
come in the window took the child away
and her all naked and covered with blood but I
went out and pushed them aside and cut her loose
and held her in my arms tender like a child
which is when she spit in my face and ran away
into the twilight into the nightmare ruins
and still lurks there in the ruins of Pendragon Castle
for all I know, to this day, laughing and singing
and moaning and screaming and grieving
turn and turn about so I got on a boat
and came across the ocean grieving always
but brought her with me in my head
she's in my head I can't get her out
and Proserpina and Magdalena
life being mostly a sequence of lost women
and somehow they know that when you look
at them you're seeing somebody else
like in the mirror at the carny house
and King George and his ragged bunch came after
like shadows the bastards had to follow me
and you will take this girl he said, or tell us

what was in that satchel at the windmill,
and them all dead and my girl Bel sits now
at the pump organ crazy as a bluejay and
her poor dumb son of a bitch of a brother a soldier
and lost in some other woman lost because
love is the deadliest poison in the world
says the angel in my head get rid of that thing
come out of her for it may love you or even worse
you may love it and either way you're lost
says the angel so I went to the crossroads by
the abandoned windmill and when some of them
gypsies or whatever the hell they was
come by and asked me what was in the bag
squirming in the bag
I said it was a badger
I got a badger in the bag,
and they looked at me and moved on,
and I left it in the windmill where the rats
no doubt – don't think of that,
and she wept in my head,
and the great claw come in the window, she said,
but she knew. I got a badger
in the bag, I said. Rhiannon.
Rhiannon. Rhiannon.

(The light fades on him and goes out.)

THE ROOKY WOOD

CHARACTERS

MOIRA
RUFFING
HOBB

SETTING

Four wooden chairs on an otherwise bare and mostly dark stage represent various locations: room, a theatre, woods. The time is the first decade of the twentieth century. The action is continuous.

"Light thickens, and the crow
makes wing to th' rooky wood;
good things of day begin to droop and drowse,
while night's black agents to their preys do rouse."
– William Shakespeare, *Macbeth*, III, ii, 50-54.

(Lights up on **MOIRA**, *a young woman, sitting on a chair, and* **RUFFING**, *a man in his forties, standing, looking at her.)*

MOIRA. I came because I thought someone should know.

RUFFING. Know what?

MOIRA. I'm sorry. I'm a little nervous. I've never been in this sort of place before.

(Pause. **RUFFING** *waits.)*

The thing is, I'm afraid.

RUFFING. What are you afraid of?

MOIRA. Well, for one thing, I suppose I'm afraid you'll think I'm not quite right in the head.

RUFFING. Why would I think that?

MOIRA. Because it is something rather odd. What I feel I need to tell you.

RUFFING. Why don't you just tell me, and let me decide if I think it's odd or not?

MOIRA. The thing is, you see, I have a kind of gift.

RUFFING. A gift?

MOIRA. Or curse. Depending on how you want to look at it. I just want you to understand.

RUFFING. Then tell me.

MOIRA. I'm trying to tell you. It's difficult.

RUFFING. Look, I'd really like to get home at a reasonable hour tonight, so if you've just come here to –

MOIRA. Someone's been killed.

RUFFING. Who's been killed?

MOIRA. A woman. I think she's rather young. My age, about.

RUFFING. Is this someone you know?

MOIRA. No. Well, I suppose it could be. But I don't think it is.

RUFFING. You're not certain?

MOIRA. I haven't actually seen her.

RUFFING. Then how do you know she's been killed?

MOIRA. I don't know. I mean, I do know, but – it's so difficult to explain. I went to a play. In the park. Shakespeare. And at intermission I took a walk by the woods. It was getting quite dark by then. And as I was passing by a certain stand of trees –

(pause)

RUFFING. What? You saw something? You heard something?

MOIRA. No. I just knew.

RUFFING. You knew what?

MOIRA. I knew that she was there. In that little stand of trees. In that part of the woods. Lying in the weeds. I just knew.

RUFFING. How did you know?

MOIRA. I don't know. I have a gift.

RUFFING. What kind of gift?

MOIRA. Sometimes I just know things.

RUFFING. So you were walking by the woods and suddenly you just knew –

MOIRA. I just knew there was a dead girl lying there naked in the woods, about twenty feet away or less.

RUFFING. How did you know she was naked?

MOIRA. I could see her.

RUFFING. You said you didn't see anything.

MOIRA. I didn't walk into the woods and see her. I saw her in my head.

RUFFING. You saw a dead girl in your head.

MOIRA. Yes.

RUFFING. You walked past a particular patch of woods in the park –

MOIRA. By the theatre. The woods by the theatre.

RUFFING. But you didn't go and look.

MOIRA. I was afraid. For all I knew, the killer could still be there.

RUFFING. But you're certain she was murdered?

MOIRA. Well, how else would she end up dead and naked in the woods? A woman doesn't generally take off all her clothes in the woods and then kill herself, does she? I think perhaps she was strangled. Or suffocated. I think she couldn't breathe.

RUFFING. How do you know she couldn't breathe?

MOIRA. I just feel it. You'll be able to tell when you find her, I expect.

RUFFING. So you somehow became convinced that there was a murdered girl in the woods near where you were walking, and then what did you do? You came directly here?

MOIRA. No. I went back and watched the rest of the play.

RUFFING. After finding a dead body in the woods you went back and watched the rest of the play?

MOIRA. I didn't actually find a dead body. I was just certain she was there.

RUFFING. Because you saw her in your head.

MOIRA. Yes.

RUFFING. You were certain, but you still went back and watched the rest of the play?

MOIRA. I was upset. I didn't know what to do. I was afraid to go and look. I needed to think. So I went back and watched the rest of the play. I didn't decide to. I just did. I thought if I told anyone, people would think I was crazy. Which I can see that you probably do. So I watched the rest of the play, and then I took a walk, to try and decide what to do. But I kept seeing that poor dead girl in my head. So finally I came here. I couldn't bear the thought of her lying naked out there in the woods all night. I knew you wouldn't believe me, at first. But I thought I owed it to her. You think I'm mentally disturbed, don't you?

RUFFING. Do you think you're mentally disturbed?

MOIRA. All you need to do is go and look. Just go and look. That's all I ask. Just go and look.

RUFFING. Come and show me.

MOIRA. I don't want to go back there.

RUFFING. If you want me to look, then come and show me.

(*Pause. She looks at him.*)

MOIRA. All right. If that's the way it must be.

(**MOIRA** *rises from the chair and walks slowly downstage as the light fades on* **RUFFING,** *who remains onstage in the dark, and comes up on* **HOBB,** *a man in his forties, sitting on one of two chairs placed side by side, facing downstage.* **MOIRA** *sits in the chair beside* **HOBB.**)

HOBB. Are you all right?

MOIRA. Pardon?

HOBB. I'm sorry, I don't mean to intrude, but I can't help noticing that you seem upset.

MOIRA. I'm fine, thank you.

HOBB. Are you sure? Because I've been studying you.

MOIRA. Studying me? You've been studying me?

HOBB. Your face. I've been studying your face.

MOIRA. When?

HOBB. During the first act. While you were watching the play.

MOIRA. While I was watching the play, you were studying my face?

HOBB. Yes. I must confess. I was.

MOIRA. Why would you come all the way out here in the woods to see a play and then spend the whole first act looking at me?

HOBB. I was hoping maybe you could explain it to me.

MOIRA. The play? You were hoping I could explain the play to you?

HOBB. No. I was hoping you could explain why I can't stop looking at your face.

MOIRA. How could I explain that to you? What do you think I am? Psychic?

HOBB. I don't know. Are you psychic?

MOIRA. I think you should just watch the play.

HOBB. I've seen the play.

MOIRA. Then why did you come?

HOBB. I felt inexplicably drawn back.

MOIRA. Then why don't you just watch it?

HOBB. Apparently because I'd rather look at you. Not just because you're beautiful – and you are very beautiful, I think, but also because something is going on in there, in your head, behind the eyes. Something very unusual.

MOIRA. Really? What is it?

HOBB. Did something happen out there by the woods? Because you seemed fine before intermission. Then I saw you walk out towards the woods there, and when you came back, you seemed upset. You really shouldn't be walking by those woods in the dark. A beautiful girl like you, all by herself, walking by those dark woods. It's very dark in there. Anything could happen. Did something happen?

(She looks at him. Lights begin to fade.)

MOIRA. The lights are going down. The second act is starting. You should watch the play.

HOBB. It doesn't matter. I know what happens.

*(He looks at her as darkness falls on them and the light comes up on **RUFFING**, standing upstage.)*

HOBB. *(Rising and moving into **RUFFING**'s light.)* I want it to be remembered that I came here of my own free will.

RUFFING. Yes, that was very good of you.

HOBB. Why do you want to speak to me?

RUFFING. Don't you know?

HOBB. I have no idea.

RUFFING. I think you do.

HOBB. *(Sitting down in an upstage chair.)* Well, you can think whatever you want, can't you?

RUFFING. I know who you are.

HOBB. Oh, really? Well, why don't you tell me who I am? I should very much like to know.

RUFFING. You're enjoying this, aren't you?

HOBB. You mean you're not? Because I've always suspected that you people get a kind of sexual pleasure from this sort of thing. It's just my theory. And capital punishment – well, there's the ultimate orgasm for you, isn't it? It's probably the reason a person goes into your line of work in the first place – a deep longing to be morally superior, and to punish. You take a sadistic pleasure from dominating the weak.

RUFFING. Are you certain you're not describing yourself?

HOBB. Even if that were true, I'd still be more honest than you. I would at least not carry with me that self-righteous veneer of hypocrisy. The truth is, any attempt to understand another person's inner life is doomed. How can you possibly be certain of another person's motives? A killer, for example. How can you know he might not kill for reasons of compassion?

RUFFING. You're putting people out of their misery? Is that what you think you're doing?

HOBB. I'm cooperating with the police. That's what I'm doing. I don't know what the hell you're doing. I mean, you call me in here, and you begin making these stupid insinuations, but you have no evidence.

RUFFING. We have a witness.

HOBB. No you don't. Why on earth do you think a man like me would go around murdering people?

RUFFING. So this wasn't the first?

HOBB. You're a very lonely person, aren't you?

RUFFING. Are you lonely? Is that why you do these things?

HOBB. You're lonely, and you feel separate from other people. You find yourself living more and more in your own imagination. Perhaps you attempt to provide yourself the illusion of company by going to the theatre, say. Do you go to the theatre?

RUFFING. You do.

HOBB. Yes, I love the theatre. But it's all vanity, of course. What we go desperately looking for in others is something we can see easily enough by simply looking in the mirror. And that, I suppose, is what theatre is, a kind of mirror.

RUFFING. What do you see when you look in the mirror?

HOBB. Investigation makes a man vulgar, doesn't it? It coarsens a person, wears him down, day by day. By constantly questioning others one is actually attempting to define himself somehow, but one fails. You are a patchwork man, a kind of scarecrow person, head filled with straw. But a patchwork quilt is also a work of art. We move through our lives, patching our quilt together with cast off fragments of truth. But for a person like you, I think there is no hope.

RUFFING. Why did you kill that girl?

HOBB. Even if I were to confess to you, how could you be sure I was telling the truth? How could you be certain I wasn't making it all up for some darker reason of my own? You really have no way of knowing for sure.

RUFFING. The proof would be that the murders would stop.

HOBB. But that's absurd. The murders will never stop. There will always be more murders. The evidence is always contradictory. There are always at least two solutions to any problem. I'm sorry, but your whole theory of justice has some very serious and ultimately fatal flaws in it. It relies upon the principle that there is a difference between right and wrong, and that human beings are capable of determining that difference, and that they're capable of determining beyond a reasonable doubt what happened someplace they weren't, or even someplace they were, and that the universe is ultimately explainable in rational terms, all of which could well be just so much rubbish. Superstition is much more honest. If you tell your children to watch out for the bogey man who lives in the ravine, even if you've never seen a bogey man in the ravine, you can't go wrong, because sooner or later there will be a bogey man in the ravine. Or in the woods. There is always some truth to folklore, but the law is always a lie, and the father of all lies, of course, is Satan, therefore the law is Satan, and the person who believes he is the law in this room is Satan. Therefore, you are Satan.

RUFFING. If I'm Satan, then who are you?

HOBB. Why, I'm Inspector Hobb, of course. Didn't you know?

RUFFING. Inspector Hobb?

HOBB. That's right. I've been investigating this case, on the trail of a serial killer, and I must tell you, Ruffing, I wouldn't be surprised if in fact it didn't turn out to be you who killed these people.

RUFFING. Me? Why would I go around killing people?

HOBB. I expect so you'll have murders to solve. And now you need to fabricate a killer.

RUFFING. You're the one who's fabricating. You're not Inspector anything.

HOBB. Why don't you go and check? Go on, Ruffing. Go and check my story. If I'm lying you'll certainly be able to determine it soon enough. What's the matter? Why aren't you going?

RUFFING. I don't need to check. I know you're lying.

HOBB. Ah, yes, that touching conviction of certainty you have. But are you certain? Are you absolutely certain you're not the killer?

RUFFING. Are you?

HOBB. I'm not certain about anything. That's the beauty of it. All possibilities are open to me. Whereas you, with your closed mind, are a prisoner of your own fabricated realities. You're trapped in a house of mirrors. You lead a very isolated life, don't you? Keeping odd hours. Obsessed with women. It's a wonder we didn't begin to suspect you a long time ago.

RUFFING. Why don't you tell me about it, then, Inspector? Tell me about how I killed all these women.

HOBB. Don't you know? Do you not remember after? I wonder if that's it. It's a part of your illness that you commit these murders and then immediately forget them. Then you wake up in the morning and go out and look for the killer. And all the while you're looking for yourself.

RUFFING. Convince me. Convince me that it's true. Tell me how it happens. I'd like to hear your theory.

HOBB. I don't believe in theories. But if I had to guess how it works, I'd guess something like this: A man goes out in the pouring rain. He has nothing in particular on his mind. He has no plan. He stops under an awning near the park. There's a woman standing there. They strike up a conversation. He's very nice, and not bad looking, and she seems to like him. The man begins to think, perhaps something will come of this. And, after a bit, something does. Or perhaps he meets her at the theatre. Or in a police station. It really doesn't matter. But I think it all rather seems each time to have been almost an accident. Of course, it never is an accident.

RUFFING. So he kills this woman, whom he's met at the police station, or at the theatre, and leaves her lying naked in the woods?

HOBB. Well, if I were a killer, I don't think I'd just leave my victim lying about in the woods. I think I should be tempted to take her home with me and have her embalmed. Some people have difficulty throwing things away. Letting things go. But that also is vanity. Everything goes away. Even embalming is only postponing the inevitable rotting of the flesh. In the end, you must learn to let things go. That is the last thing we learn.

RUFFING. But why does the killer do it? I want to understand why he does it.

HOBB. To stand under an awning in the rain with a woman
who is not unattractive and to become aware, gradu-
ally, that something is possible. That something could
happen. I imagine it's an extraordinary feeling. We go
through our lives half asleep most of the time. And
then suddenly, for a moment, something causes us to
wake up. To look with new eyes. We realize that time
is – that certain moments – that one can, that it is possible to – Suppose a man suddenly became so curious
about the mystery of things, he had to see what was
inside. He had to see. And there she was, in the rain.

(pause)

You look like you could use a drink, Inspector.

RUFFING. Do you want a drink?

HOBB. It might loosen my tongue a bit.

RUFFING. All right.

(**RUFFING** *takes out a flask, passes it to* **HOBB**.)

HOBB. *(unscrewing the cap, wiping off the top)* Lord love a
duck.

(He drinks.)

Ah. My brand as well. You identify with me, don't you?

RUFFING. Identify with you?

HOBB. You identify with me, and you envy me.

RUFFING. Why would I envy you?

HOBB. Because I have tasted the red blossoms of her
breasts.

RUFFING. Whose breasts?

HOBB. What most people are too stupid to realize is that
there is also poetry in Hell, and every place is haunted.
Every human soul is haunted. There is always something lurking in the weeds. Have you ever been in a
mental ward?

RUFFING. Have you?

HOBB. I understand one has vivid and very troubling dreams, in a mental ward.

RUFFING. Dreams about what?

HOBB. There are no mirrors in such places, you know.

RUFFING. Why is that?

HOBB. So you can't look in the mirror and see somebody else. Or the Devil, just over your shoulder.

(pause)

Doing this makes you feel important, doesn't it?

RUFFING. Does killing innocent people make you feel important?

HOBB. I don't know any innocent people.

RUFFING. Is that why you kill them? Because you think they're guilty of something? Some sort of original sin?

HOBB. The touch of flesh to flesh is an extremely powerful stimulus. In India of course they have certain ones who are untouchable. A person habitually lonely, like yourself, craves contact, but fears it. Touch is a very powerful weapon. Women know this.

RUFFING. And you resent them for it?

HOBB. I don't resent women. I honor them. I consider them goddesses. I worship them. Every chance I get. What do you do with them? Do you perhaps take them out into the woods?

*(**RUFFING** looks at him. Lights fade on **HOBB** and come up on **MOIRA**, standing in the woods. Wood sounds. Night.)*

MOIRA. Here, I think. Very near here. We're very close now. I think we are.

RUFFING. *(Stepping into her light.)* I thought, with your remarkable psychic powers, you'd be certain. You're not certain?

MOIRA. I'm confused. It doesn't feel the same. Something is getting in the way. I don't know what it is. It's like something is giving off, sending out – it's like there's a very powerful interference suddenly, in these woods. I don't know.

RUFFING. Are you telling me you can't find her now?

MOIRA. I don't know. Maybe she's not here any more. Maybe somebody found her, or maybe the murderer came and took her away somewhere.

RUFFING. Or maybe I've come out here to the woods in the middle of the night in search of a dead girl who was never here in the first place.

MOIRA. She was here. Maybe she's still here. Look, I'm not crazy. At least I don't think I am. It's like, to me it's like remembering. But I'm remembering somebody else's past. Something vivid and terrible. Or it could be something trivial. Or something that seems trivial to me but was once for some reason terribly important to somebody else, like a photograph that's a treasure to one person but rubbish to another. What makes a thing valuable, a memory, an object, a person, even, is what somebody has felt about it, about them. It's emotion that makes value. And memory. Without memory there is no value. It's not like I want to be this way. It's not like I want to know these things. It just happens.

RUFFING. Then why isn't it happening now?

MOIRA. Sometimes I can only see what I don't want to see.

RUFFING. This is useless. I'm going home and get some sleep.

MOIRA. Wait a minute.

RUFFING. What?

MOIRA. I'm getting something.

RUFFING. Now that I'm leaving you're getting something.

MOIRA. Shut up. Just shut up a minute.

(pause)

It's a memory. I don't think it's a dream, but I'm not certain. There's a child, a little boy, and he's walking in the woods, and he's quite happy, but then he discovers that he's lost, but at first he's not too troubled by this. And then he stops and listens, trying to figure out which way to go, and then he can feel a sudden eerie sensation that he's not alone, or rather, the sensation that one feels when one is for the first time deeply, so deeply alone that one is completely disoriented – it's like dreaming but also waking from the dream that one's life has been, and standing there in the the middle of the woods this boy begins to panic, chills, the hackles at the back of his neck rise, his bowels constrict, he's breathing harder, his heart is pounding, it's panic – forest panic – unexpected overwhelming irrational terror in the woods, named for the sudden eerie awareness of the presence of the dead god Pan. Panic. And the boy begins to run. He's terrified. And then he stumbles over something.

(pause)

RUFFING. What? What does he stumble over?

MOIRA. You know, don't you?

RUFFING. I don't know. Tell me. What does the boy stumble over in the woods?

MOIRA. It's the body of a young girl. Quite naked. Lying in the woods. She's been strangled.

(pause)

It's yours, isn't it? It's your memory.

RUFFING. What is this?

MOIRA. It happened to you. Or you dreamed it. Or it happened to you and now you dream it, over and over again. And sometimes, at night, you go out, and walk in the night.

RUFFING. What place have you brought me to? Why have you brought me to this place?

MOIRA. There are clocks in the boy's head.

RUFFING. There are no clocks in the boy's head.

MOIRA. There are clocks. I can hear clocks.

(pause)

RUFFING. My father made clocks. His shop, in our house, was a clockworks maze, a labyrinth of ticking clocks.

And all the clocks said different times. They would chime away madly at all hours, you never knew when. All the clocks said different times. And sometimes I would get up in the middle of the night and go down into the shop and listen to them ticking and ticking everywhere, and the hackles on the back of my neck would rise. It was like the beating of a thousand little hearts.

(pause)

MOIRA. It's me.

RUFFING. What is?

MOIRA. I've seen the face of the dead girl lying naked in the woods. It's my face. It's me. I was seeing my own death. That's what I was seeing. I'm lying there naked and dead in the middle of the woods.

RUFFING. Where?

MOIRA. Here. Right here.

(pause)

It's beginning to rain.

RUFFING. Yes.

MOIRA. Are you going to kill me now?

(pause)

RUFFING. You're the psychic. You tell me.

(Pause. She looks at him. Sound of ticking clocks as lights fade to darkness.)

DUTCH INTERIORS

CHARACTERS

VERMEER

(Lights up on **VERMEER**, *speaking from a room in Delft.)*

VERMEER.

I bought it from van Hoogstraten, one of his perspective boxes. The bastard is very clever. There are two little peep holes you can look in. Your choice. What you see when you peep into the perspective box is a view of a set of rooms in a house that looks vaguely familiar – a cozy and inviting but also somehow vaguely sinister Dutch interior.

Seen from the outside, it's just a dark wooden box. But when you look in the peep hole, the illusion is so powerful, you have a hard time believing the house you see is just a few cleverly painted panels inside a box. You embrace very quickly the illusion that the house stretches back into much deeper space than the size of the box. And you lose all sense of the actual size of the box, for how can you know if a thing is large or small if you have no outside point of reference? It's as if contained in that little box was another dimension, another universe, folded inside our own, but vast, unfathomable.

Paintings, of course, often give one the sense of having stumbled upon an alternative reality, but the perspective box is more than a painting, because once you press your eye to the peep hole, your eye has become a location within a three dimensional universe. You are in that room. You are in that house. You can see through half open doors down corridors that lead to other rooms. I can't stop looking into this box. The rooms haunt me. I dream about these rooms. And I have this eerie feeling I was dreaming about these rooms long before I ever looked in this box. It's as if that smug son of a bitch van Hoogstraten had somehow captured the place I dream of and put it in this box.

The rooms inside this box bear an uncanny resemblance to the rooms of my father's inn, where I grew up. The rooms and corridors, the staircases and half opened doors, the checkerboard floors and chairs, all remind me so much of the place, it can't be a coincidence. Yet why would van Hoogstraten pick my father's inn, of all places, to reproduce inside his perspective box?

It's not as if we're any sort of friends. Rivals, more often. Van Hoogstraten doesn't think much of my paintings, and frankly, I don't think much of his, ordinarily. But this perspective box is different. The thing that's always annoyed me about van Hoogstraten is that he sees art as a kind of trick, a deception, which art most definitely is not, and he is not really a very imaginative fellow, either, all in all, and yet the bastard has created this amazing, hypnotic object which has already cost me I don't know how many hundreds of hours of work, and a great deal of grief from my wife, who is usually a bit more tolerant of my many small vices, and my mother-in-law, who thinks I'm an idiot.

What on earth, they said, are you spending the last of your money on a wooden box for? And of course I had no answer for them. There is really no way I could possibly make them understand the immense power this box has over me. I look into it for hours, until the rest of my body seems merely a kind of useless appendage to my right eyeball, the eyeball that connects me to the peep hole through which I enter the magical world of the perspective box.

Then one day, when I'd been staring into the perspective box for so long I'd lost all sense of time, I thought I saw something moving way back there in the far room by the staircase. At first I was convinced it must be my eyes getting blurry from too much staring, or perhaps some insect had somehow got into the box. But the next day I saw another bit of movement, just past the half-opened door on the left. My God, I thought. Somebody is in the perspective box house. I became obsessed with getting a glimpse of this person. I spent more and more hours each day staring into the perspective box. My wife was very concerned, and my mother-in-law was convinced that I'd gone mad, like her poor son Willen, who believes that the devil lives in his mother's cuckoo clock.

The next day I looked in the box and there was the girl, just her back at first, until she turned to gaze in my direction, and the moment I saw her eyes, I was lost, utterly lost. Her beauty sucked every bit of breath out of my lungs. A young girl, shy and a bit sad, wearing a pearl earring. She turned and looked over her shoulder at me in the most compelling and enigmatic way, and my heart stopped beating. Time stopped. And then she turned away and disappeared through the door and into the maze of half-hidden rooms at the back of the perspective box house.

The moment she was gone, I was impaled by grief and torn with doubt. Had I really seen her? Of course, in art, as in love, neither grief nor doubt is unfamiliar. While one is totally immersed in the act of creation itself, there is no doubt. The doubt begins the moment the paint dries. Doubt concerning the identity of the creator. Doubt concerning the identity of the subject. Doubt concerning the identity of the artist's model. Is it a forgery? Is it not what it appears to be? Is it not what it appears to wish to appear to be?

Having myself descended from a long line of frauds and con men who were very much wedded to disorder, who changed their names frequently and lived disorderly lives in disorderly Dutch houses, and given that all our ancestors, good and bad, live on inside us, jabbering quietly in our heads like demented ghosts, my first instinct was to suspect that van Hoogstraten must have somehow lured me into some sort of elaborate con game by selling me a trick perspective box designed to drive me to distraction.

I looked in the box again. The girl with the pearl earring was nowhere in sight. Had I simply been hallucinating? I was peering into the box, trying desperately to look into corners and down hallways to catch a glimpse of the girl again, when I felt a sudden sharp pain, as if an arrow had been shot into my buttocks. I cried out and turned to discover my mother-in-law, who had whacked my behind with an egg separator.

Will you stop gaping into that stupid box and do something, for God's sake? she said. All you seem to be good for is making my daughter pregnant. At least, I presume you're the one responsible for that. Personally, I can't imagine how she can bear to let you touch her. She could have married a rich pig farmer in Utrecht, but no, she had to have an artist. And not just any artist, but one who takes three years to finish a painting. How can you ever hope to finish anything if you spend all your time with your eyeball pressed to that damned peep hole? What's the big fascination with that box, anyway? It's just a box. How can you look into it hour after hour all day and half the night? You're loonier than my poor son Willen, who spends all day staring at the cuckoo clock, waiting for the devil to come out. At least a bird comes out of the clock once in a while. What the hell does that stupid box do?

How could I explain to her what I'd discovered? How could a good, respectable, stupid woman like herself begin to comprehend what I'd stumbled upon? I couldn't understand it myself. I promised her I'd try to work harder, but it's difficult, with my children constantly galloping back and forth through this big, disorderly house in Delft like a herd of antelope, chasing kittens and emitting earsplitting shrieks. The house is full of cats. I don't know why the house is full of cats. Who ordered all these damned cats?

There is a cat sitting in one of the rooms of the perspective box. On the back wall, there's a painting of a seascape. A boat on a calm sea. A patch of yellow in the View of Delft. All things have meaning, but the meaning moves about from one emblem to another, like the cat moves from one room to another in the house. There are emblems nested inside emblems. A palimpsest of emblems, the iconography of mental incunabulae. The picture on the wall contains a picture on the wall, and everything is done with mirrors.

Every emblem is a puzzle, but the explanation is not the solution, for an essential element of the emblem is ambiguity. Why should a man be disturbed to find images signifying one thing in one case and something else in another? I am speaking to the cat, who sits by the fire and stares at me. The response of the cat is ambiguous, but not meaningless. Am I dreaming or am I awake? Am I in or out of the perspective box? And which is the dream? Which is the illusion?

There is a letter on the floor of the perspective box. Was it dropped there by the girl? Is it a letter for me? A love letter, dare I hope? For I am desperately in love with the girl with the pearl earring. She looked at me again today. What is she thinking? What does she see when she looks at me? A picture on the wall? It is so enormously frustrating not to be able to get myself deep enough into this box to touch her. Oh, God, how I long to kiss her lips.

I can hear a splashing of water. Is she bathing? Is she naked, just out of my sight, just on the other side of the doorway? If only there were a mirror on the wall, so I could see the reflection of her naked flesh, just a glimmer of bare flesh reflected in a mirror would mean everything to me. I can see the edge of the bedclothes move. Has she crept naked into bed? I believe I will go insane with desire. And yet it is much more than desire. She is somebody in my soul.

Camera obscura: a device by which light is trapped and a scene formed upside down upon a wall through a tiny hole. Matter, said my friend van Leewenhook, is composed of small globules, just like your paintings. There are universes within universes, he says, looking into a drop of water. But has van Leewenhook ever fallen desperately in love with a creature he sees in a drop of water?

The girl with the pearl earring stands at her window, reading the letter. Is it from the soldier I have seen her laughing with? Has he abandoned her? This officer wears a stupid hat and puffy sleeves that make him look like a sissy. But he makes her laugh. He has been to all the places on the map behind her. At least, he says he has. And she chooses to believe him, because it amuses her to choose this. But now she is with child by him, and he has abandoned her.

I mourn as she does. The soldier is so cruel. Van Hoogstraten, you sneaky bastard, what have you done to this poor child? Poor little de Hooch people. Checkerboard floors. I think there is much, much grief concealed in these Dutch interiors. This grief has worked its way into my nightmares. I am dreaming her memories now. Skating on the frozen canal in winter, when the hunters come up suddenly over the horizon. A great painting, like a great love, is a trap we can never escape. We are trapped in the painting forever, as in a glass ball.

How painters die: a meditation. Fabritius met a noble painterly end. He was doing a portrait of the sacristan when the powder magazine blew up. Ignis fatuus, from the Latin words for fire and foolish. A light seen at night moving over swamps or marshy places, believed to be caused by the combustion of gases arising from organic matter. Popularly called will-o-the-wisp, or jack-o-lantern. A deceptive hope, goal, or influence. A delusion. All dark backgrounds recede.

She reads her letter at the open window, a tear form-
ing in her eye. Her reflection in the glass. Spilled
fruit on the bed. The eternal drop cloth again, which
looks suspiciously like my own. Madness. To be able to
touch. I want to see, but seeing is never enough. I want
to touch her flesh. I want to touch. And yet if I take
the box apart I will destroy it. This is what God will do
at Armageddon. He will disassemble the perspective
box he has put us in.

A patch of yellow which is something else. There are
numerous small changes on the rooftops. The image
created is not the thing itself. It is pictures within pictures, mirrors reflecting mirrors. What does it mean?
How does one begin to extract meaning from love, or
a work of art? What sense can it possibly make to one
outside it?

I paint the people I see in the perspective box, to try
to make sense of what I see, to get closer to it, by telling myself stories about their lives. But these stories
are no more true than the stories I tell myself about
my own life, which has been largely imaginary, except
possibly for all these goddamned cats.

Is she turning back to me, or is she giving me one last
look before she turns away forever? I will never know
for sure. Her haunted eyes. Her mouth, which I will
never kiss. Her shoulder. To slip the robe gently off
her shoulder. Her chin. Her neck. Her breasts naked
before me. Slip off her turban and her strawberry hair
will fall down onto her shoulders. Oh, God, oh, God,
oh God.

But she does not want me. I am nothing to her. A picture on the wall. She is infinitely far away from me, like
the light from a galaxy which no longer exists. And yet
she is right here in this little box. And she is looking at
me. Oh, God, her eyes, her eyes.

Planning does not signify. You must catch the moment
as it comes. This letter which, breathing in spring air,

is read over many times, the bowl of fruit on the bed, the brown light and where the officer has gone. His death, for which I am perhaps responsible, a powder magazine has mysteriously exploded and – calm. I must be calm.

Her reflection in the dark glass. The child that stirs within her. The seed in the fruit on the bed. Hidden behind the curtain, the rotting officer is whispering jokes about love. Is the girl with the pearl earring mad? Or is it somebody else? There is so much I don't understand. Why does she hold the book and the trombone? And why does there sometimes seem to be foliage growing from her head? In the labyrinth of emblematic iconography, something always remains hidden. The images must be distorted to maintain the illusion of depth. The images must be –

What is art if not an attempt to lose one's self in another world by making that world or by being absorbed completely into the world another has made? To blend one's inner experience so completely with that of another is the deepest form of intimacy. But what if one has in fact created the other? But in love, as in art, one has always created the object of one's attention. What use are candle and spectacles if the owl refuses to look?

The cat is staring at me. Crows caw in the little court-yard outside my window. I can hear the distant voices of children running through the house. One day my mother-in-law will come into this room to look for me, and find it empty. Then, curious, she will look through the peep hole in the perspective box. Will she see me in there?

I dream that I'm wandering lost in a desolate landscape filled with windmills, and somebody seems to be shooting at me. I come upon a house that looks familiar, a kind of inn, go in a door, and find myself inside the perspective box.

I hear a splash of water in another room. The girl with the pearl earring is taking a bath. I am trembling. I move towards the bedroom, down a corridor I have stared at for hours from outside the box. But now I am folded within her labyrinth. When I pass into this half opened door, I will see the girl naked in her bath. I will see her, and she will recognize me, and I will comfort her, and raise her child as my own, and we will be lovers forever. I reach out my hand to push the half open door. But just then I trip over the cat and fall, hitting my head against the bulldog doorstop, and wake up in my own bed. The damned stupid cat is sitting on my chest, staring into my eyes. I push the cat away, rush to the perspective box and look in, and there is the girl with the pearl earring, looking over her shoulder at me. Is it accusation in her face? Have I betrayed her somehow?

I can't sleep now. I want desperately to dream this dream again, to get back inside the perspective box, to hold her and comfort her. But when I doze off, I dream instead that I am falling into the vanishing point. I will plummet hopelessly into this darkness forever. I close my eyes and scream, but nobody hears me. Lost. I am utterly lost.

But then, at the darkest point of my despair, I open my eyes and I'm once again inside the perspective box. It is the future, and the perspective box has sat forgotten in the storage room of a museum for hundreds of years. I wander the rooms of my perspective box prison, looking for the girl with the pearl earring, but I can't find her. Then, on a table in one of the back rooms of the perspective box, I find another perspective box. I look in the box and there she is, looking back over her shoulder at me. Is she turning towards me, or is she turning away? Does she beckon me?

(The light fades on him and goes out.)

.

FRENCH GOLD

CHARACTERS

DAVID ARMITAGE, 70
MOLLY RAINEY, 50, his half-sister
LIZZY HOPKINS, 55, his half-sister
BECKY PALESTRINA, 23, their niece

SETTING

The tangled and overgrown garden at the center of the old Pendragon house just outside of Armitage, a small town in east Ohio, on an autumn afternoon in the year 1950. An old bench in a rose arbor, and some old Victorian wooden chairs. The set should be as simple as possible.

(The tangled and overgrown garden at the center of the old Pendragon house just outside Armitage, a small town in the hilly part of rural east Ohio. The house is very old, and over the years has been built completely around the garden, which is now overgrown with bushes and trees. An old bench in a rose arbor, not far from a sundial which we need not see. An autumn afternoon in the year 1950. **DAVID ARMITAGE**, *age 70, sits on the bench. Sound of birds singing at dusk. Then his half-sister,* **MOLLY RAINEY**, *age 50, appears, looks at him for a moment.)*

MOLLY. I suspected I'd find you here.

DAVEY. You're a clever girl, Molly.

MOLLY. If I'm a clever girl, what am I doing married to Cletis?

(She comes over and sits down beside him.)

This garden is a mess. It's not even a garden, I don't know why we still call it that, it's just trees and overgrown bushes and that old broken sundial. All these little paths and weeds. God only knows what lives in here. There's probably snakes in there as big as Vermont. It's a wonder you don't get lost in all this tangle, Davey.

DAVEY. I've always been partial to labyrinths. And I like the garden this way, surrounded by the house. There's some comfort in being able to get lost without leaving home.

MOLLY. We ought to clean it up.

DAVEY. There's nothing wrong with a little disorder.

MOLLY. This isn't a little disorder. This is a horticultural catastrophe.

DAVEY. Well, I like it.

(pause)

MOLLY. I don't know what we're going to do without Sarah. She's been here all our lives. All my life, all Lizzy's life. She kept the family together more than anybody, and she wasn't even related to us. At least, not that I know of. Kinda hard to tell with us, sometimes. I don't know what we're going to do.

(pause)

What are you going to do, Davey?

DAVEY. I expect get older for a while and then die, at some point.

MOLLY. But who's going to look after you, with Sarah gone?

DAVEY. I'll get along all right.

MOLLY. Who's going to cook?

DAVEY. I can feed myself.

MOLLY. You don't want to be alone out here in this big old falling down monstrosity of a house, Davey.

DAVEY. Where exactly do you think I should want to be?

MOLLY. You could come and stay with us. Now that Becky's married and got her own house, we've got the apartment upstairs empty.

DAVEY. I like it here.

MOLLY. Or you could stay with Lizzy.

DAVEY. Lizzy's got Dorothy.

MOLLY. I could take Dorothy.

DAVEY. Dorothy drives you crazy.

MOLLY. I can handle Dorothy. I just don't think it's healthy for you to be rattling around this big old mausoleum all by yourself.

DAVEY. I'm fine, Molly.

MOLLY. I don't think you're fine.

DAVEY. Just stop fussing at me.

MOLLY. I'm not fussing at you.

DAVEY. You're always fussing at me. You've got to learn how to let things alone sometimes.

MOLLY. I don't want to let things alone.

DAVEY. That's what I'm saying.

MOLLY. What we should really do is sell this good for nothing old dump once and for all and be done with it.

DAVEY. We're not selling this place.

MOLLY. Then what are we going to do?

DAVEY. We're going to let things alone.

MOLLY. You know, Davey, in your own way, you're the most stubborn son of a bitch in the whole family.

DAVEY. I'm going to take that as a compliment.

MOLLY. Somebody ought to cut down that tree.

DAVEY. Leave that tree alone.

MOLLY. It's going to fall on the house.

DAVEY. Not today it isn't.

MOLLY. Fine.

(Pause. LIZZY appears, age 55.)

LIZZY. There you are. Hiding in the crab apple rose arbor. It's like the elephants' burial ground out here.

MOLLY. Is everybody gone?

LIZZY. No, I'm still here. Lewis is waiting and Dorothy is looking for the cat. Did you and Davey talk about that thing we talked about?

MOLLY. Davey likes it here.

LIZZY. I can't see why. It was nice when we were girls, but it was falling apart even then. Now it's a disaster.

DAVEY. I think it's beautiful.

LIZZY. For Dracula, maybe. I'm not sure it's even safe.

DAVEY. Nothing is safe.

LIZZY. The whole thing could fall down on top of you like the House of Fisher.

DAVEY. Usher.

LIZZY. What?

DAVEY. The House of Usher. Not Fisher.

LIZZY. Well, one of them houses. You could fall through the floor into the potato cellar and never be seen again.

DAVEY. That's exactly how I want to go.

LIZZY. You ought to go live with Molly.

DAVEY. I don't want to live with Molly.

LIZZY. I don't see why not.

DAVEY. Would you want to live with Molly?

LIZZY. I'd rather be drawn and quartered.

DAVEY. Well, there you are.

(*pause*)

LIZZY. We ought to cut down that tree.

DAVEY. WILL YOU JUST LEAVE THAT GODDAMNED TREE ALONE?

LIZZY. All right, all right. You don't have to bite my head off.

(*pause*)

And that stupid sundial. That thing proves all the Pendragons were crazy. Who would build a sundial in the shade?

MOLLY. Well, Lizzy, I expect it wasn't in the shade when they put it here.

LIZZY. It's been in the shade since we were little girls.

MOLLY. That tree was probably fifty years old when we were little girls. I expect that sundial was there before the house grew around the garden. Zach Pendragon put that sundial there.

LIZZY. Well, he was crazy, wasn't he? Didn't he kill somebody?

MOLLY. I don't know if he did or not.

LIZZY. I seem to remember he killed somebody.

MOLLY. That was long before our time.

LIZZY. Not that long. Time makes me itch.

(*pause*)

It doesn't feel right here without Sarah.

MOLLY. No.

LIZZY. She wasn't just a housekeeper. She was the heart of this place.

MOLLY. That she was.

LIZZY. Who's going to take care of Davey now?

DAVEY. Will you two stop talking about me as if I was a three year old? I am not an invalid. I am not feeble minded.

LIZZY. You're a writer. You need somebody normal to take care of you. The real world isn't your sort of place, Davey.

DAVEY. I've seen a good deal more of the real world than either one of you have, and, on the whole, I like it here just fine, so let me grow old here in peace, and leave that tree alone.

LIZZY. I worry, is all.

DAVEY. You worry too much.

LIZZY. Not just about you.

MOLLY. She worries about Becky.

LIZZY. I worry about Becky.

MOLLY. And Becky's children.

LIZZY. And Becky's children.

DAVEY. Becky's children are fine.

LIZZY. I don't know about that. June and Lorry are rather alarming little girls.

DAVEY. What's wrong with them?

LIZZY. They tried to mail the baby to Europe.

DAVEY. No they didn't.

LIZZY. It's true. Becky found them putting him in a box and wrapping it up. They said they were sending him on a trip to France.

DAVEY. France is beautiful this time of year.

LIZZY. Not if you're a baby wrapped in a brown paper package. They're going to kill that poor little boy.

DAVEY. He'll be all right.

LIZZY. It could scar him for life. He's half Pendragon and half Italian. That's two strikes against him already.

DAVEY. Ben will be fine.

LIZZY. This garden is a mess. You could get lost in here.

DAVEY. I've been trying to, but you people keep finding me.

LIZZY. What's going to become of this place?

MOLLY. I don't know. Time is a pretty ruthless customer, Lizzy.

LIZZY. I'm telling you, some day this whole place is going to collapse in a heap, just like that story Father read to us.

MOLLY. What story?

LIZZY. The story about the house. And there was a dead girl, only she wasn't dead. And the house collapsed at the end. Their name was Fisher.

MOLLY. Sounds like a wonderful story.

DAVEY. "The Fall of the House of Usher." It's "The Fall of the House of Usher."

LIZZY. No, I don't think that was it.

DAVEY. Well, if the house falls in, I want to be here.

LIZZY. It isn't healthy to live alone.

DAVEY. Everybody's alone.

LIZZY. Not me.

MOLLY. I wish I was, but I got Cletis.

BECKY. *(calling from off)* Hello? Where is everybody?

MOLLY. There's Becky.

BECKY. Where the hell are you people?

MOLLY. Don't tell her.

LIZZY. Over here, Becky.

BECKY. Where?

LIZZY. Here.

BECKY. Where?

LIZZY. Here.

BECKY. I can't see you .

MOLLY. We're over here by the sundial.

BECKY. What?

MOLLY. The sundial.

BECKY. I don't see any sundial.

MOLLY. That's because you're not here.

BECKY. Where?

MOLLY. Where we are.

BECKY. Where are you?

MOLLY. By the sundial.

DAVEY. Becky is lost.

MOLLY. She's always lost.

LIZZY. It's not her fault. She fell on her head.

BECKY. *(appearing)* There you are. Who fell on their head?

LIZZY. Nobody.

BECKY. Are you telling people how I fell on my head again? Why are you always telling people that?

LIZZY. Well, you did fall on your head.

MOLLY. We thought you went home.

BECKY. Uncle Lew made me help Aunt Dor chase Sarah's dumb old cat, and I got lost out here, and now we can't find Aunt Dor, either.

MOLLY. Your husband thought you left without him.

BECKY. I got lost. I always get lost here. I hate this place. It gives me the creeps.

LIZZY. We'll give you a ride home, Becky. Johnny took the children.

BECKY. That stupid cat. It won't listen to anybody but Sarah. I don't know what's going to happen to it now.

DAVEY. I'll take care of it.

BECKY. Are you staying here?

DAVEY. I'm staying here.

BECKY. Why in God's name would anybody in their right mind want to stay out here?

DAVEY. I like it here.

BECKY. Weird.

LIZZY. Don't call your uncle Davey weird.

BECKY. He's a poet. That's not weird?

LIZZY. It's not polite to call people weird.

DAVEY. I used to be a poet. Then I was a cryptographer. Now I just make imperfect translations from dead languages to living ones that will probably be dead themselves soon enough.

BECKY. Uh huh. Great. Can we go now?

LIZZY. Why don't you come with us, Davey?

DAVEY. No thanks.

LIZZY. Just for tonight?

DAVEY. I'm all right.

LIZZY. I don't want to go off and leave you all alone out here tonight after we just buried poor Sarah and the cat's missing and I just don't know what to do about you.

DAVEY. You don't have to do anything about me, Lizzy. I'm a grown up person. I can take care of myself. You just go on.

BECKY. Uncle Lew says we can't go until we find Aunt Dorothy.

LIZZY. Well, where is she?

BECKY. We don't know. She went after the cat and disappeared. Maybe her and the cat made a break for it. I wish I could.

LIZZY. All right. Davey, I put most of the left over food in the refrigerator.

DAVEY. Fine.

LIZZY. I wish you'd remember to eat once in a while.

DAVEY. I'll remember.

LIZZY. Sarah used to say if she didn't grab you and hogtie you and drag you to the table, you'd never eat anything.

DAVEY. Sarah could have had a great career in the rodeo.

LIZZY. Well, a person's got to eat.

BECKY. Can we just go ? I don't want to leave the girls alone with the baby. I'm afraid they'll drop him on his head.

LIZZY. Why don't you come with us, Davey? You can play checkers with Cletis.

DAVEY. I don't want to play checkers with Cletis. He cheats.

LIZZY. Cletis doesn't cheat. He just can't see.

MOLLY. No. He cheats.

DAVEY. Go away, Lizzy.

LIZZY. I just know some day I'll come out here with a pan of chicken and find you dead in the garden, with Sarah's cat eating you.

BECKY. Icck. Aunt Liz. Can we just go? June and Lorry are going to throw the baby out the window, I just know it.

LIZZY. They're not going to throw the baby out the window.

BECKY. Last week they were sliding him down the laundry chute like a watermelon.

LIZZY. Johnny will take care of the children. You stay here and keep your Uncle Davey company while Molly and me go find Dorothy.

BECKY. I don't want to stay here with him.

LIZZY. Becky.

DAVEY. I don't need company.

BECKY. See? He doesn't need company.

MOLLY. He's a man. He doesn't know what he needs.

BECKY. I want to go.

MOLLY. Well, you can't go until we find your Aunt Dorothy, and if you go looking for her you'll just get lost again. You never could find your way around this place, so you just stay here and try to be civil to your Uncle Davey. Is that too much to ask?

BECKY. Fine.

MOLLY. Fine. Let's go, Lizzy.

LIZZY. Davey, if you need anything, you just give us a call, all right?

DAVEY. I will.

LIZZY. No you won't. Stubborn. I swear. Becky, be nice.

(**MOLLY** and **LIZZY** go off. Pause.)

BECKY. I hate this place.

DAVEY. Yes.

BECKY. I didn't mean to be rude.

DAVEY. I know.

BECKY. Sometimes things come out of my mouth and it's like somebody else is saying them, you know?

DAVEY. Yes.

BECKY. I don't really think you're all that weird.

DAVEY. Well, you know, to call a poet weird is not necessarily an insult. It comes from a Scottish term that describes a sense of fate or mystery, a kind of odd seeing into things. That's really what poets do.

BECKY. Uh huh.

(pause)

Stupid cat.

DAVEY. What?

BECKY. Sarah's cat. It's always running away. I've been trying for fifteen years to make friends with that cat, and it always runs away from me.

DAVEY. You can't chase cats. You've got to let cats come to you.

BECKY. But it doesn't come to me. It runs away.

DAVEY. That's because you chase it.

BECKY. But I wouldn't have to chase it if it didn't keep running away.

(pause)

How can you stay all alone out here? I mean, even when Sarah was alive, it must have been really lonely and creepy out here, but now, with just you and the damned cat – I just – how could you stand that? Don't you like people?

DAVEY. I like people.

BECKY. Then why do you run away from them?

DAVEY. I'm not running. I stay put. They come to me. Just like the cat.

(pause)

BECKY. What's a cryptographer? Did you like, work in a crypt or something?

DAVEY. Well, kind of, but no, not the way you're thinking. During the war my job was to try and decode German messages.

BECKY. Really?

DAVEY. Yes. The Nazis sent messages to each other in a very difficult code, and I spent a lot of time trying to break the code so we could figure out what they were saying.

BECKY. But I'll bet you never figured it out, did you?

DAVEY. No, actually, we did figure it out.

BECKY. You did?

DAVEY. Yes. We did.

BECKY. Wow. How did you do that?

DAVEY. Trial and error, mostly. It took a long time. But it was an interesting problem, and it did some good, in the end, I think.

BECKY. I thought you were a soldier.

DAVEY. In the first war I was.

BECKY. Aunt Liz said you got medals and things.

DAVEY. A lot of people did.

BECKY. I think war is stupid.

DAVEY. You're absolutely right.

(pause)

BECKY. What's keeping them? Stupid cat. I got to get out of here.

DAVEY. They'll find Dorothy pretty soon. The cat, I don't know.

BECKY. I don't just mean this house. I got to get out of this town. This state. I really got to get out of here.

DAVEY. Are you and Johnny thinking of moving?

BECKY. No. Just me.

DAVEY. You want to leave your husband?

BECKY. No. I don't know. I love my husband. But my children drive me crazy. And sometimes I just – I don't know. I get this itch in my head and I start to feel like the walls are closing in on me, and Aunt Liz and Aunt Molly are picking at me, and the children are screaming, June and Lorry are throwing the baby back and forth like a football, and Uncle Lew is always trying to tell me what to do, and Aunt Dor is always staring at me, and the cat keeps running away – it's like there's all these people in my life making me lonely and driving me crazy, and sometimes I just want to get the hell out of this place and never come back. Did you ever feel like that?

DAVEY. Yes.

BECKY. No you didn't.

DAVEY. I did get the hell out of this place. But then I came back.

BECKY. Why did you come back? God, if I ever escaped from this town I swear I'd never come back.

DAVEY. I think I just ran out of places to hide. That's what home is. When you've run out of places to hide, that's where you end up.

BECKY. I might just go. I might just take off and go.

DAVEY. Where would you like to go?

BECKY. I don't know. Actually, no place. If I went someplace else, I'd just want to be back here. I have what I wanted. I have a great husband. I have a nice house. I have three children. No troubles to speak of. And sometimes I'm really, really happy. But it doesn't stay. It stays for a second and then this thing starts to flap like a bat in my brain, it's like there's this little rat running around in my head, and I just, I'm restless, and I can't think, I can't concentrate, and everything annoys me, and I just feel like –

(pause)

BECKY. This garden. Who the hell builds their house all the way around a garden? It's like all this weird vegetation is growing up through the house. It's so weird. I hate that. Uncle Clete says there's gold buried here. He says there's French gold buried in the garden. But I think it's a bunch of crap, like all Uncle Clete's stories. How the hell would French gold get to this place, anyway?

DAVEY. Well, the story is, when the French held Fort Duquesne, before it was Pittsburgh, during the French and Indian wars, some Frenchmen headed west when the English were coming to take the fort, and they had all the gold they'd collected there, and when they got out here in the middle of nowhere they buried it, someplace close to where Zach Pendragon built his mansion, and the Frenchmen died before they got back to dig it up again, so the treasure's still here.

BECKY. Do you believe that?

DAVEY. Oh, I don't know. I'm a poet. I'll believe anything.

BECKY. If you're a poet, why don't you write poetry?

DAVEY. I promised a woman.

BECKY. What woman?

DAVEY. Somebody a long time ago.

BECKY. Promised her what?

DAVEY. I said I'd give it up for her.

BECKY. Oh.

> *(pause)*

Was she impressed?

DAVEY. I don't know. I never saw her again. That was my first lesson about love.

BECKY. I don't understand.

DAVEY. That's the lesson.

> *(pause)*

BECKY. Where is she now?

DAVEY. I have no idea.

BECKY. Is she dead?

DAVEY. Quite possibly.

BECKY. But you still don't write poems.

DAVEY. No.

BECKY. How long has it been?

DAVEY. Not long. Less than forty years.

BECKY. I can't even keep my head focused on one person for six months, and you've been loyal to a dead woman for forty years. Wow. Maybe I did fall on my head.

DAVEY. Becky, you know, however restless your brain is, however unsatisfied with your life you might be, and I'm not saying that you ought to just settle for something you don't want, but you know, you might not have forty years. You might not have forty minutes. It's quite an accomplishment just to behave like a decent person for two minutes. I'm just working on those next two minutes. And your children – difficult as they may be, still – that it's possible for life to happen, for new beings to be formed out of us and grow into people before our eyes – that has a value not to be cast away lightly.

BECKY. It's hard. Why is it so hard?

DAVEY. Because it matters.

BECKY. I don't understand why I do things. I don't understand why I feel things. I don't know what's going on in my head. It's like the inside of my head is a foreign country. I don't even understand the language.

DAVEY. Cryptography. All things are written in cryptograms. Life and death are a labyrinth of cryptographic symbols, magical formulas we can no longer decipher. And my friend Sarah lies now under fresh earth. I don't know what to make of that. I never have.

BECKY. Sarah didn't like me.

DAVEY. Of course she did.

BECKY. No. She didn't. She thought I was selfish and useless. She spent her whole life taking care of several generations of people in this family, and she got nothing for it. She died a lonely old woman in the wreckage of a house she spent her whole life trying to keep from collapsing onto the messed up people who lived there. She liked to take care of people. I guess it was all she had. But I hate it. I mean, I like animals better than children, and children better than people, but sometimes I just hate everything that can make you care about it. I just want to get the hell away from it. And this place just keeps reminding me of it. This place is full of ghosts.

DAVEY. Every place is full of ghosts. And all beloved things are lost, eventually. You can't change that by running away.

BECKY. You ran away.

DAVEY. I ran away from here, to escape this place and all its ghosts, and then I ran back here, to escape what I found when I got to wherever the hell it was I thought I went to. But this place was where I went to, and where I went to was always here in this demented garden surrounded by the labyrinth of the house where my father brooded once upon his betrayals, where generations of our kind have made love, died, and come to mourn. Something is buried here, something we can't quite get to, something very close that we just can't see. I am slowly turning into my ancestors. We always turn into the people we try to escape. You will too.

BECKY. Not if I get the hell out of here first.

DAVEY. There is no other place. The wind blows leaves about in the Sibyl's cave in all possible combinations, but no journey is to anyplace but back. Time moves in one direction on the surface, devouring as it goes, but inside it's always moving backwards to the past. All we can do is hold on to the people closest to us in the labyrinth, pass on whatever love is possible from each to the next, as best we can. It's buried deep inside us, the capacity to love unreasonably, hopelessly, no matter what. It's there, like lost French gold. Sarah knew. Sarah loved you.

BECKY. Sarah's gone.

(Pause. Then the truth of what she's just said hits **BECKY**, *and tears begin to roll down her face. The wind blows some leaves about.* **BECKY** *cries quietly for a moment, then wipes her eyes and looks up.)*

BECKY. That's kind of a nice old tree, isn't it?

DAVEY. It's a beautiful tree.

*(***BECKY*** *puts her head on Davey's chest.* **DAVEY** *holds her. Leaves blow about in the garden. The light fades on them and goes out.)*

Among the most frequently published and widely produced playwrights in the world, Don Nigro has continued to build a deeply inter-related but remarkably diverse body of dramatic literature over the years, work that is often mysterious and unclassifiable, employing a wide variety of dramatic conventions and styles of presentation. He has written monologues and epics, spare realistic dramas and surreal homicidal puppet farces, plays with music and verse plays. He continues to build the long cycle of Pendragon County plays, which traces the history of America through the lives of several related east Ohio families from the eighteenth century to the present, and features many characters whose lives are followed from youth through middle-age to old age in a number of plays designed to be presented in a variety of different combinations. Nigro has twice been a finalist for the National Repertory Theatre Foundation's National Play Award, and has won a Playwriting Fellowship Grant from the National Endowment for the Arts and grants from the Ohio Arts Council and the Mary Roberts Rinehart Foundation. He has twice been James Thurber Writer in Residence at the Thurber House in Columbus.

His work has been translated into French, Italian, Spanish, German, Polish, Greek, Russian and Chinese. John Clancy's production of Nigro's *Cincinnati,* featuring Nancy Walsh, won Fringe First and Spirit of the Fringe awards at the Edinburgh Fringe Festival, Best of Fringe at the Adelaide Fringe Festival, and has toured Britain. *Seascape With Sharks And Dancer* has been in the repertory of Teatr Syrena in Warsaw, and *Lucia Mad* was produced at Teatr Julius Slowakie in Krakow and the Teatro del Fantasma has presented a Spanish translation of *The Girlhood of Shakespeare's Heroines* in Mexico City. *Widdershins* was produced as part of the first International Mystery Festival. Nigro's plays have also been produced in Singapore, Hong Kong and Beijing, and toured India. SpielArt, based in Munich, has translated and toured two productions of his plays in Germany.

His work is produced every year in a variety of New York

theatres, and has been done at the Oregon Shakespeare Festival, the McCarter Theatre, Actors Theatre of Louisville, Capital Repertory Company, the Hypothetical Theatre, the Berkeley Stage Company, Manhattan Class Company, the People's Light and Theatre Company, Theatre X, Shadowbox Cabaret, the Hudson Guild Theatre, the WPA Theatre, and many others, in every state.

Born in 1949 in Canton, Ohio, Nigro grew up in Ohio and Arizona. He has a BA in English from The Ohio State University and an MFA in Dramatic Arts from the Playwrights Workshop at the University of Iowa. Nigro has taught courses in Comparative Literature, Dramatic Literature and playwriting at Ohio State, Iowa, Kent State, Indiana State, and the University of Massachusetts at Amherst. *Grotesque Lovesongs* was translated and produced on Polish television, and the film *The Manor*, with Peter O'Toole, is based on his play *Ravenscroft*. Forty-eight volumes of his plays have been published by Samuel French. The Don Nigro Collection at the Jerome Lawrence and Robert E. Lee Theatre Research Institute at the Ohio State University contains a growing repository for his manuscripts and other materials.

Also by
Don Nigro...

Anima Mundi
Animal Salvation
Ardy Fafirsin
Armitage
Autumn Leaves
The Babel of Circular
  Labyrinths
Ballerinas
Balloon Rat
Banana Man
Barefoot in Nightgown
  by Candlelight
Beast with Two Backs
Bible
Binnorie
Boar's Head
The Bohemian Seacoast
Boneyard
Border Minstrelsy
Broadway Macabre
Capone
Captain Cook
Chronicles
Cincinnati
Cinderella Waltz
The Circus Animals'
  Desertion
Creatures Lurking in
  the Churchyard
Crossing the Bar
The Curate Shakespeare
  As You Like It
The Dark Sonnets of
  the Lady
The Dark
The Daughters of
Edward D. Boit

The Dead Wife
The Death of Von Horvath
Deflores
The Devil
Diogenes the Dog
Doctor Faustus
Dramatis Personae
Dutch Interiors
Fair Rosamund and
Her Murderer
Fisher King
Frankenstein
Genesis
The Ghost Fragments
The Girlhood of
Shakespeare's Heroines
Give Us a Kiss and
Show Us Your Knickers
Glamorgan
God's Spies
Gogol
Golgotha
Gorgons
The Great Gromboolian Plain
Great Slave Lake
Green Man
Grotesque Lovesongs
The Gypsy Woman
Haunted
Hieronymus Bosch
Higgs Field
Horrid Massacre in Boston
Horse Farce
Ida Lupino in the Dark
The Irish Girl Kissed
in the Rain
Joan of Arc in the Autumn

The King of the Cats
Laestrygonians
The Last of the Dutch Hotel
The Lost Girl
Loves Labours Wonne
Lucia Mad
Lucy and the Mystery of the
Vine Encrusted Mansion
Lurker
MacNaughton's Dowry
Madeline Nude in the
Rain Perhaps
Madrigals
Major Weir
The Malefactor's
Bloody Register
Mariner
Mink Ties
Monkey Soup
Mooncalf
Mulberry Street
My Sweetheart's The
Man in the Moon
Narragansett
Necropolis
Netherlands
Nightmare with Clocks
November
Paganini
Palestrina
Panther
Pendragon
Pendragon Plays
Picasso
Quint and Miss Jessel at Bly
Ragnarok

Ravenscroft
The Reeves Tale
Rhiannon
Ringrose the Pirate
Robin Hood
Scarecrow
Seance
Seascape with Sharks
and Dancer
The Sin-Eater
Something in the Basement
Sorceress
Specter
Squirrels
Sudden Acceleration
Sycorax
Tainted Justice
TheTale of the Johnson Boys
Tales from the Red Rose Inn
Things That Go Bump
in the Night
The Transylvanian Clockworks
Tristan
Uncle Clete's Toad
Warburton's Cook
The Weird Sisters
Widdershins
Wild Turkeys
Winchelsea Dround
Within the Ghostly
Mansion's Labyrinth
Wolfsbane
The Wonders of the
Invisible World Revealed
The Woodman and the Goblins

Please visit our website **samuelfrench.com** for complete
descriptions and licensing information